"Liattraction between us,"

Josh said.

"Yes, we can."

"You propose to just ignore it, then?" Josh asked.

"There's nothing to ignore," Lindsay answered.

"Are you trying to tell me you didn't feel anything back there on that rock a few minutes ago?"

"We...we had a wonderful day together. Can't... can't we just leave it at that?" Lindsay asked.

A wonderful day together. Yes, it had been. Lindsay had made it wonderful. But leave it at that? Forget one minute of it? He could easier fly. "Okay, Lindsay, we'll play it your way. We'll live under the same roof, see each other every morning, every night. We'll smile at each other, brush past each other in the hallway, and we'll pretend there's nothing between us." Josh turned Lindsay to him, tilted her chin up and gave her a kiss, long and deep and stirring. Then he pulled away and smiled into her glazed eyes. "We'll forget it all."

Dear Reader,

Summer may be over, but autumn has its own special pleasures—the bright fall foliage and crisp, starry nights. It's the perfect time to curl up with a Silhouette Romance novel.

This month, we continue our FABULOUS FATHERS series with Nick Elliot, the handsome hero of Carla Cassidy's *Pixie Dust*. Under the influence of a little girl's charms and a mother's beauty, even a sworn bachelor can become enchanted by family life.

Love and miracles are alive and well in Duncan, Oklahoma! This little town with a lot of heart is the setting for Arlene James's brand new trilogy, THIS SIDE OF HEAVEN. The series starts off this month with *The Perfect Wedding*—a heartwarming lesson in the healing power of love.

In Elizabeth Krueger's *Dark Prince*, Celia Morawski accepts Jared Dalton's marriage proposal while tangled in the web of her own lies. But is it possible her prince has secrets darker than her own?

Be sure not to miss the fiery words and sizzling passion as rivals fall in love in Marie Ferrarella's *Her Man Friday*. Look for love and laughter in Gayle Kaye's *His Delicate Condition*. And new author Liz Ireland has lots of surprises in store for her heroine—and her readers—in *Man Trap*.

In the months to come, look for more books from some of your favorite authors, including Diana Palmer, Elizabeth August, Suzanne Carey and many more.

Until then, happy reading!

Anne Canadeo
Senior Editor
Silhouette Books

HIS DELICATE CONDITION
Gayle Kaye

Published by Silhouette Books New York

America's Publisher of Contemporary Romance

If you purchased this book without a cover you should be aware that this book is stolen property. It was reported as "unsold and destroyed" to the publisher, and neither the author nor the publisher has received any payment for this "stripped book."

To my mother, Ethel Sondergard—my biggest fan.
Thanks for all your faith in me.

 SILHOUETTE BOOKS
300 East 42nd St., New York, N.Y. 10017

HIS DELICATE CONDITION

Copyright © 1993 by Gayle Kasper

All rights reserved. Except for use in any review, the reproduction or utilization of this work in whole or in part in any form by any electronic, mechanical or other means, now known or hereafter invented, including xerography, photocopying and recording, or in any information storage or retrieval system, is forbidden without the permission of the publisher, Silhouette Books, 300 E. 42nd St., New York, N.Y. 10017

ISBN: 0-373-08961-9

First Silhouette Books printing September 1993

All the characters in this book have no existence outside the imagination of the author and have no relation whatsoever to anyone bearing the same name or names. They are not even distantly inspired by any individual known or unknown to the author, and all incidents are pure invention.

®: Trademark used under license and registered in the United States Patent and Trademark Office and in other countries.

Printed in the U.S.A.

Books by Gayle Kaye

Silhouette Romance

Hard Hat and Lace #925
His Delicate Condition #961

GAYLE KAYE

had a varied and interesting career as an RN before finally hanging up her stethoscope to write romances. She indulges this passion in Kansas City, Missouri, where she lives with her husband and one very spoiled poodle. Her first romance in 1987 reached the finals of the Romance Writers of America Golden Heart contest.

When she's not writing, she loves to travel or just curl up with a good book.

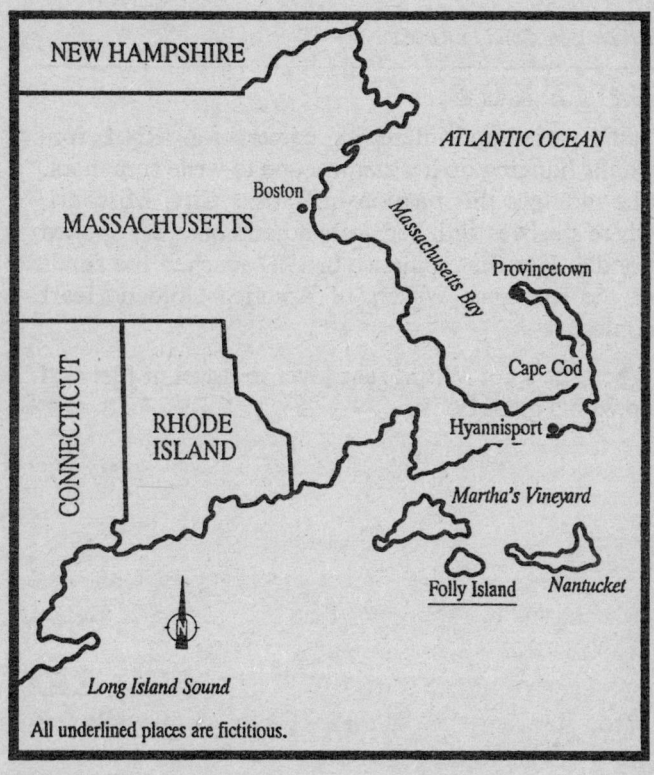

Prologue

"One week," Josh Alexander said, frowning at the two men who were his friends from college as well as his partners in the successful firm of Bainbridge, Alexander and Bailey, Financial Consultants.

"Two weeks," Tom Bainbridge came back. "That's the agreement. Two weeks on the island with total isolation from the financial world. You're not even to read the *Wall Street Journal*."

"That's right," Cliff Bailey, the quietest of the three, joined in. "Cold turkey, Josh. It's the only cure for a workaholic."

"Unless, of course, you're ready to admit defeat now," Tom gibed. "Admit you can't do it—you can't relax for a measly little two-week vacation."

"Piece of cake," Josh retorted. He started to drum his fingers impatiently on the polished surface of the conference table but caught himself in time. "I'm going to win this bet, and then you two will pay off handsomely."

"You should thank us for this," Cliff added. "You're looking at heart-attack city by age thirty-five if you keep up this pace. Happens to guys in this business all the time."

"And you're trying to keep me from being a statistic. Your kindness overwhelms me." As he spoke, he swept up a sheaf of papers from the table and slid them into his Moroccan leather briefcase. "Now, if this meeting's over..."

"Hold it. Those papers stay here," Tom snapped, taking control of the briefcase. "As of this moment you're officially on vacation."

"Terrific," he said. He seized the briefcase back from Tom's hands. "I'll drop this in my office and be on my way."

"Er, that's another thing," Cliff spoke up quickly after exchanging a conspiratorial glance with Tom. "We're escorting you to the ferry landing—just in case you get some bright idea to fly to the island instead of the leisurely trip by water."

Two hours on the slow-rocking ferry! He'd go insane. "Don't trust me, guys?" he asked with a wry smile.

"Not in the least," they agreed in unison.

Josh speared them with a frown and strode out the conference room door.

"Is everything set?" Cliff asked as soon as Josh was safely out of earshot.

"All set. Got him booked into the Cottage Rose, the quietest place on the island and run by a doting spinster. Oh, I almost forgot. To ensure Josh doesn't try to cheat on the deal, I sent a letter to the proprietress, telling her that he has a serious heart condition. Even reading the stock market reports could trigger an attack."

Cliff chuckled long and hard. "He'll be bored out of his brain."

Chapter One

Lindsay Mills stuffed the latest batch of bills into a cubbyhole in the old oak rolltop desk. She just couldn't worry about them today. She had guests arriving. One this afternoon, three tomorrow. The Cottage Rose would be full for the first time since she'd taken over after her great-aunt's death two years ago.

Rose had had a way with people, catering to their every whim and pampering them silly, but she'd been a poor business manager. Lindsay wasn't sure there was enough red ink on the island to do the inn's books. But this season promised to be different. If she could keep the guest rooms full for the summer, and if the old plumbing held for another year, she could put the place in the black.

She'd been hesitant about confirming the last guest, a Joshua B. Alexander. He had a heart problem, no doubt an elderly gentleman and one who apparently liked to play the stock market. But the check for his full two-week stay, along with a hefty bonus for looking after him, had been just too tempting to refuse. And retired Doc Tobias, who lived a stone's throw from the Cottage Rose, said he'd be available in the event of an emergency. She'd posted Doc's number and the number of the island's small ambulance service next to the phone.

She'd even moved her things upstairs to the tiny third-floor bedroom, giving the gentleman the one on the main level. The frilly pink and rose hues she'd redone it in might be a bit too feminine for him, but he would be better off not having to climb steps with his aging ticker.

Lindsay gave a quick glance at the antique grandfather clock in the front parlor. She still had two boxes of her things to move upstairs to her new room and just enough time to do it before she had to leave for the ferry landing to pick up Mr. Alexander. It was a service she liked to provide for all her guests and one she was certain Aunt Rose would have approved of heartily.

If she had time, she wanted to stop by Doc's and pick up the old wooden wheelchair he'd said she could borrow for the duration of Mr. Alexander's stay. She didn't know if the man would need it, but it was best to be prepared just in case.

Pleased that she'd thought of everything, she went to retrieve the boxes. They weren't heavy, just cumbersome, both of them full of her paints and blank canvases, supplies she most likely wouldn't have a chance to touch until the summer tourist season ended. She'd be too busy squeezing orange juice for breakfast, keeping the linen laundered, the guest rooms cleaned and answering the myriad of questions about the island that her guests thought up. But, if she got the opportunity, she would escape to one of her two private spots: the widow's walk atop the house, which commanded a view of the entire island as well as a goodly distance out to sea, or the deserted stretch of dunes where she could paint for hours.

Unable to see around the boxes in her arms, she felt for the bottom step with the toe of her pink espadrille and started up the old curved staircase. Halfway to the first landing she heard the front door jingle open.

Who was here?

Someone hoping for a vacancy, no doubt, and this week she didn't have as much as a broom closet available. She turned around for a glimpse of her visitor, but as she did, the top box shifted.

"Oh, no!" Lindsay squeezed her eyes shut as the box began its descent. She waited for the crash, envisioning burnt umber and madder blue congealing on the polished wood floor at the bottom of the stairs. Instead of the expected crash, she heard a very male *"Ooooph!"*

Her eyes flashed open to find that capable hands had caught the traveling box in mid-plunge. Above the box was a pair of impressively wide shoulders. Her gaze roved upward to his face, hoping it would be a familiar one, not the face of a prospective summer guest, visions of lawsuits dancing in his eyes.

He was not familiar—but he was definitely handsome. Disconcertingly handsome, she amended. Her heart beat rapidly.

His hair was black and curly, his eyes dark as sin—and hooded as if he were very tired. An overworked mainlander, looking for a little R and R, she decided, summing him up in her usual race-to-conclusion manner. If it weren't for the signs of fatigue—or stress—in those few tight lines bracketing the edges of his mouth, his full-shaped lips would be downright sensual. Right now he looked too tired to pucker.

And it was safer that way, Lindsay decided wryly. Fully rested, the man was no doubt dangerous.

He'd apparently dropped his navy suit jacket on the floor next to a bulging tan suitcase, when he'd made his well-timed lunge for the box. A red silk power tie, its knot yanked open, hung around his neck, and the top three buttons of his light blue shirt were undone.

"Where do you want this thing?" he asked, climbing the stairs to the same step she stood on. He motioned for her to load her box on top of the one he held.

There was an intensity in his eyes that nearly frightened her. She obeyed, settling it onto the one in his arms. "I was taking it to the third floor, but you can just set it on the landing."

She followed him up the stairs. "I'm sorry I don't have any vacancies," she said. "That is what you came for, isn't it?"

He didn't stop at the landing but climbed higher. His face looked pale in the light that danced through the small, round window where the old stairway curved upward to the next floor. And he was perspiring lightly—whether from the exertion or the warm day, she didn't know.

"I already have reservations," he said, continuing upward.

Lindsay followed behind. "Oh. Where are you staying?" Folly Island was much smaller, less touristy, than its sister islands, Nantucket and Martha's Vineyard. There was only a scattering of places with accommodations.

"Here." He turned and smiled, a smile that eased his tired facial lines. Not even the apparent stress he was under could daunt its brilliance. "This is the Cottage Rose, isn't it?"

Lindsay stared up at him. "There must be some mistake," she said. "I only have one guest arriving today, and you aren't—"

"Where should I put these?" he asked, reaching the third floor and eyeing each bedroom in turn.

Lindsay caught her breath at the top step. "Oh—uh—there." She pointed toward her new room, a half room really, tucked away under the eaves of the weathered centuries-old house. "Anywhere on the floor will be fine."

He parked the boxes in the center of the room, then stepped back out into the hallway. "Josh Alexander," he said, extending his hand.

She stared at him. "Not...not Joshua B. Alexander?"

"'Fraid so."

Oh, Lordy! Realization hit Lindsay like bricks raining from the sky. Joshua B. Alexander wasn't an old man with a heart condition, he was a young man with a heart condition. And she'd nearly bumped him off, letting him tote those boxes.

"The stairs... You... you could have had a heart attack," she said, as the enormity of it all hit her anew.

One dark eyebrow raised like a question mark. "A heart attack?"

She nodded.

His eyes narrowed at her. "You sound like my partners. I'm in good shape—maybe working a little too hard, but that's all."

Lindsay gave him a good once-over. He towered over her on the third-floor landing, his rock-hard chest and well-muscled shoulders directly in her line of vision. She could hardly fault his shape. But what did that prove, other than he had a good body? It didn't prove his ticker wasn't on the fritz.

The letter from his associates had clearly stated that he would try to deny he had a heart problem. And she could understand that. He was still young, probably only a few years older than her twenty-nine years.

She couldn't discount that faint sheen of perspiration dotting his forehead. And she was sure there was a paleness to his face. She needed to get him downstairs where the light was better, but maybe he should rest first.

Yes, rest, that's what he needed.

She shoved him toward the small blue velvet settee on the landing. "It's best to learn your limitations, Mr. Alexander."

"Limitations? I don't have any limitations. There's nothing wrong with my heart—or any other part of my anatomy, for that matter. And I really wish you wouldn't call me Mr. Alexander."

It wasn't good to get him upset, she realized. A vein stood out on his temple—not a good sign. "All right—Joshua."

"Josh. I prefer Josh."

"Josh, then." Placate the man. When Doc heard what she'd done, letting an ill man lug two boxes up to her room, his thick old mane of hair would turn whiter than it already was.

Her guest refused to stay seated, but stood up from the settee. "Tell me," he said, his voice sounding like thunder in the small space, "just how did you get the impression there's anything wrong with my heart? I'd like to know."

Lindsay had a few questions of her own, such as how he'd gotten to the island so early. The Carrie Belle didn't dock for another hour and she doubted he'd swum the thirty miles from Hyannis. But that could wait.

"Why, from Mr. Bainbridge and Mr. Bailey, of course—when they made the reservations for you. They seemed most concerned."

His face was growing red and his jaw clenched until she thought it would snap. "You really need to relax," she told him. "You're far too uptight. This island is a restful place. You can keep to a slow pace here. It should be perfect for you."

Just as Josh had suspected. His partners had set him up. Well, he was getting out of here right now. Maybe he could still catch the charter pilot before he gassed up and returned to Hyannis. His friends had nearly foiled his plans when they'd insisted on escorting him to the ferry landing, but as soon as they'd dropped him off, he'd hailed a cab and beat it over to the airport to catch his charter. He couldn't stand the damnably slow ferry and he couldn't stand two weeks on quiet Folly Island.

He didn't care that the woman who'd appointed herself both guardian and nurse of his supposedly ill body was the most delightful thing he'd seen in a long time or that she made his heart thump as erratically as if he really did have a heart condition.

Did she know how delectable she looked in that striped pistachio tank top and those tight-fitting white shorts she was wearing? Her hair was silver blond and worn in a long braid down her back. Eyes the color of a blue-green wave dancing in the sunlight peeked out from beneath gold-tipped lashes.

He didn't care if he lost this ridiculous bet. No, he decided on second thought, that wasn't quite true. If he could prove to his partners that he could relax for two weeks, he'd win—they'd go along with his plans to open that second office in Boston. And if he could get them to go along with that, he intended to convince them a third one in New York would make Bainbridge, Bailey and Alexander even more successful—a name to be reckoned with.

That was important to him. It meant everything to him.

He drew a deep breath. He'd have to stick it out. Besides, his partners would laugh themselves silly if he hightailed it back to the mainland on the very first day. Who cared if this woman thought he was ready for a trip to the coronary care unit, his life hanging by a precarious thread. There could be some side benefits to that.

He looked over his pint-sized landlady. A smile tilted his lips. She could be just the incentive he needed to survive this bet. "Why don't you show me to my room," he suggested. "I should settle in and, ah, get some rest."

"Oh, yes, certainly."

He followed her down the staircase, admiring the way her backside jiggled enticingly in those shorts. Perhaps his partners were right—he needed to take the time to enjoy some of the finer things in life. "What sort of relaxation do you recommend for my first day on the island?"

He wanted to really get into this.

She turned and slanted her face up to him. A decidedly feminine scent wafted upward to tease at his senses, a whisper of something floral and hypnotic. "There's a huge old hammock out behind the inn. It's the perfect place to read a book. And there's a collection of mysteries in the glass-fronted bookcase near the front desk."

"Mysteries." How long had it been since he'd taken the time to read anything beside financial journals. "Do you serve lemonade?"

"I can stir up a pitcher."

"Great."

They'd reached the first floor. "I've put you in the back bedroom," she said. "That way you won't have any stairs to climb."

Of course. His condition. She was being thoughtful and that touched him. He doubted very much he could convince her that the exercise would do him good. He hadn't had the time to spend at the gym lately—not with the long hours he put in. Well, he'd have nothing but time here on the island. He might as well get in a little physical fitness—but he'd have to indulge out of sight of his landlady.

"Do I have a view?" he asked, thinking how very much he was enjoying the one in front of him at the moment.

"A view? Well, yes, of sorts." She smiled up at him. "If you stand on the window seat and peer out over the oleander bush in the backyard, you can just glimpse the ocean in the distance."

"I'll remember that." He wondered how much his partners were paying for two weeks of glimpsing the ocean over an oleander bush. He hoped it was a lot.

"I'll just get your bag. You can sign the register." She shoved a small paisley book at him.

Josh picked up the pen attached to the book by a satin ribbon and dashed off his name and address, then turned to find his landlady struggling with his luggage.

"I, uh, think I'd better carry that. It's too heavy for you," he said. She stood about five-two, maybe three, and probably weighed a hundred pounds soaking wet. His male imagination toyed with that last thought. In that tank top *soaking wet* could be an interesting concept. "It's full of big binders—work I have to go over while I'm here."

She dropped the suitcase instantly. "*Work!* But you can't do that."

"I can't?"

"The letter from Mr. Bainbridge expressly said you were to relax while you were here, that any sort of work could be dangerous."

"What Mr. Bainbridge doesn't know won't hurt him," he said with a sly smile. He reached for the suitcase.

"I'm quite capable of carrying a little luggage," she insisted. "Besides, your heart—"

Their hands met on the handle. Josh felt a sudden jolt of awareness. Her hand was warm under his, her skin soft. Her scent teased at his nostrils.

"My heart will be fine." He wasn't so sure about his libido at the moment, however. And he was having trouble breathing. He wrestled the bag away from her. "Just, uh, show me to my room."

She dragged her hands to her hips in a huff. "You know, you really should be more concerned about your condition. Your friends are worried about you, but you don't seem to care a fig."

His *friends* wanted him to have a stress-free vacation—no, a boring vacation—and had gone to great lengths to see that he did. He opened his mouth to tell her just that, but she turned and started down a narrow hallway, presumably toward his quarters.

He followed behind, content to watch the way her long braid swung to and fro above her firm derriere. Obviously his partners had never seen the petite proprietress of the Cottage Rose—or they'd have sent him to Outer Mongolia, instead.

"Here we are," she said, indicating a big, spacious room to her left. "There's a bath attached, with an oversized, claw-footed tub." She looked him over as if she were measuring him for it, then crossed the room and parted the curtains to let in the afternoon sun.

He hefted his suitcase onto an antique luggage rack and joined her at the window. "Is that the oleander bush?" He pointed to a pink, blossoming shrub.

She glanced out the window, then back at him. "So the room doesn't have a view," she said frostily. "The upstairs bedrooms do, but you don't need to be climbing stairs, not in your condition."

His heart again.

He could try to tell her the truth, but he suspected the woman was an innocent, locked away on this remote island. In addition, his partners had done a number on her. How would he ever convince her he was as sound as a dollar?

"I'd suggest you get unpacked—except for those binders that feel like bricks in your suitcase—and take up residency in that hammock for the rest of the afternoon." She pointed to the object in question swinging between two tall island maples. Thick green leaves formed a bower above it, patches of sunlight dappling through.

Lying in a hammock might not be so bad. A man could content himself there for hours, dreaming of... "Does that offer of lemonade still hold?"

She smiled then, a shy smile that came and went like a warm, fluttery breeze, making him want to see it again.

Often.

"It does," she said, as if he were a man who'd finally come to his senses. "I'll meet you in the backyard."

* * *

She would have felt safer had Josh Alexander been pushing eighty as she'd expected, Lindsay decided, gazing through the ruffle-curtained kitchen window at the man stretched out in her backyard hammock. He looked like he was straight out of an L. L. Bean catalog in the khaki safari shorts and black knit T-shirt he'd changed into. A light ocean breeze played with the ends of his thick, dark hair, mussing them provocatively.

She dragged her gaze away and squeezed the living daylights out of a defenseless lemon. She'd gotten more than she'd bargained for with this man. He didn't seem to understand the seriousness of his situation at all, refusing to accept his condition. A definite case of denial. She'd have to talk to Doc about it.

She poured the fresh squeezings into a tall glass pitcher, added a moderate amount of sugar, then water and stirred furiously. Against her will her gaze flickered out the window again. The spoon clinked in the pitcher. It was hard to believe that anyone who looked that virile, that gorgeous...that *healthy* could have anything seriously wrong with him. But then, in the high-stress game he was in, even young men had heart attacks, she knew.

She plunked down the spoon, poured a full glass, added a sprig of fresh mint and shoved her way through the screen door.

Perfection, Josh thought as he watched Lindsay cross the grassy lawn toward him. Then he eyed the single glass of lemonade in her hand. "I thought you'd join me."

She smiled briefly. "I have an inn to run."

Of course, he thought. Managing the Cottage Rose single-handedly, she was no doubt busy. So much for his hopes of her playing nursemaid to his purportedly ailing body.

She was as bright as sunshine, and he didn't want her to leave. Her scent reminded him of a fresh, blooming flower garden, the same scent that permeated everything in the bedroom he'd checked into. It was Lindsay's room—and she'd given it up to him. Now all he had to do was figure out how he was going to get to sleep in that four-poster bed at night when her presence there was as strong as an uninvited ghost.

"Stay," he urged. "Tell me about the island. After all, if I'm gonna spend some time here, I'd like to know what there is to do." Besides lie here in this hammock, letting the ripple of ocean breezes waft over him. Paradise. And he was trapped here in enforced isolation.

"This is a quiet island."

Just as he feared. Probably not a fax machine on the— "Newspapers. Does the island get newspapers from the mainland?" Josh could feel himself breaking out into a cold sweat. He had to know just how isolated this place was.

"Of course we have newspapers." She sat down on the grass and hugged her knees. "They're a day late, but we get the *Boston Globe,* the *New York Times*—"

"The *Wall Street Journal?*"

"I don't know. It's not on my usual reading list, but you're not supposed to be poring over the financial papers, anyway. You're supposed to be relaxing."

Ah, yes, relaxing. "Television? You do have TV? Cable—the financial channel?"

She shook her head. "The inn doesn't have a TV." Lindsay had never installed one, and she didn't intend to. "The Cottage Rose is supposed to be an escape from the outside world, a place to experience unadulterated rest and relaxation."

Josh groaned. His friends had thought of everything, fixed his wagon but good. "Unadulterated R and R."

"Yes."

"I'll get bedsores if I lie in this hammock every day."

"It does leave little marks on the skin."

Josh raised a leg to inspect the phenomenon. Sure as hell, there were little squares trying to make permanent indentations on his legs. Terrific.

Lindsay couldn't help herself. Her gaze ran over the length of Josh's extended leg and his straight, even toes. The rest of his body wasn't bad, either, she thought, unable to resist a quick perusal. With a little tan he'd be completely devastating.

Then she glanced at his face and saw that he was enjoying her checking him out as if he were ripe fruit in the supermarket. A blush climbed up her cheeks to take up residence there. "I'd better be getting back inside," she said.

"Don't leave me here," he said in rising panic. "Not until you tell me what there is to do all day."

"Oh." That was one of her duties and she would be remiss if she didn't outline a few activities for the man, she supposed. "Well, let's see, there's—"

"How about offering me a tour of the island," he suggested hopefully. He'd enjoy having Lindsay to himself for a while. "On the way in from the airport I noticed a place that rents bicycles. We could—"

"Do you have a death wish or something?" Lindsay stared at him in disbelief. "Bicycling is a great way to see the island, yes, but not for a man in your condition."

He forgot he was supposed to be ill. He flopped back onto the hammock that was beginning to feel more and more like an invalid's bed and stared up at a sunbeam glistening through the leafy maples. "I guess that does rank right up there with climbing stairs."

"Yes, it does."

"I don't imagine I can convince you my doctor thinks a little exercise each day is good for me."

Lindsay considered this. "I could check it out with Doc Tobias," she said, "but only after you've had a few days to rest and get some sun."

"Doc Tobias?"

"Yes. Doc is a good friend. He lives down the road."

Josh wondered if the man could be bought. For the first time since he'd gotten to Folly Island, he began to see a glimmer of hope.

Chapter Two

Josh had tried.

He'd spent the better part of thirty minutes in the backyard hammock, letting his mind wander, listening to the birds chirp, doing absolutely nothing at all after Lindsay had gone off to tend to whatever duties an innkeeper had to tend to.

The longest thirty minutes of his life.

Now he wore a groove in the hardwood floor in his room, pacing its length to keep from going quietly insane. He couldn't relax. It wasn't in him to relax. He was a Type A personality and Type A's did not relax—*ever*. He suspected that the few who tried promptly dropped dead from the inertia. Or their families were visiting them in the loony bin.

He did not want to meet the same fate.

His mind gave one last, fleeting thought to this relaxation thing—putting his feet up, unwinding, letting his mind run on idle—but it was hopeless. In a heartbeat he crossed the room and flipped open the lid of his suitcase. From under a few pairs of socks and boxer shorts he unearthed half a dozen binders, work he'd smuggled out of the office under the judicious eyes of his determined partners. Among his shirts he found his trusty laptop computer and set it up on the scarred antique desk in the corner.

His gaze shot to the door as if he expected his pert landlady to waltz in at any moment, find him and send for the paramedics. But it didn't happen. All was quiet in the house. Too quiet. The whole damn island was quiet, isolated from the rest of the world.

He cleared off a spot on the desk and set to work. He could lose himself for hours in a good stack of financial reports.

He was ambitious. Okay—overly ambitious. But there was nothing wrong with that. His partners enjoyed afternoons off, weekends off, Mondays off, Fridays off. It wasn't that they didn't carry their fair share of the work load. In their own laid-back manner of doing business they did.

But Josh operated at a different speed—fast forward. And he didn't apologize for it. It had worked well for him for years, and he didn't feel like changing, saw no need to change, didn't know what he'd do with himself if he tried to change.

He thrived on competition. Always had. He supposed that came from being raised in a family of males—six Alexander sons, competing with each other from the day they were born. It had been bred into him. He had goals, a timetable for success from which he never deviated.

By ten o'clock he needed a break. He had read through the latest stack of financial journals and stock reports that he hadn't had time to go over in the office the past few weeks. He'd fed facts and figures on various company portfolios into his laptop. He'd worked straight through the dinner hour, which was nothing unusual for him. Pushing Save on his laptop, he stood up to stretch his cramped muscles.

That was when he caught a whiff of warm cinnamon. It came from the kitchen—Lindsay's kitchen. If his nose served him correctly, his landlady was baking.

His stomach gave a rumbly groan. He wasn't sure if it was hunger pangs or thoughts of the enticing Lindsay that propelled him out of his room and down the hall toward the delicious aroma.

She had her hands dug into pastry dough, halfway to her elbows, when he found her. A full red apron covered the front of her, but her backside was visible for his full enjoyment. His gaze ran over its curvy shape in her well-fitting white shorts, lingered a lengthy moment on her straight, tanned legs, then slowly traveled upward again. She worked at the dough intently as if she were punishing it for something, and he wondered briefly what that something might be.

There was a light sprinkling of flour dust on her arms and one provocative smudge on her right cheek. He leaned against the doorjamb and unabashedly watched while she worked.

And to think he'd spent the best part of the evening in his room doing paperwork when he could have spent it here, admiring this delectable beauty do the baking. He watched awhile longer, taking in her deft, feminine motions, then finally announced his presence with an unsubtle cough.

Lindsay's head snapped around at the sound. She thought she was alone, absorbed in her task, but her newest guest smiled at her from the doorway. He looked all male, with the evening shadow of a beard darkening his face and frank appraisal in his eyes.

The man was going to be trouble, she was sure of it. Just his wide, brilliant smile had the power to unnerve her, send her thoughts skittering off in every direction. She tried to ignore him and the magnetic tug his presence had on her senses and concentrate on getting another batch of rolls baked for breakfast, but she was failing miserably.

"Can I do something for you?" she asked more sharply than necessary.

She was doing quite enough for him already, Josh realized as she fastened that clear blue-green gaze on him. Her eyes were wide and expectant, the kind of eyes a man could drown in if he wasn't careful.

Josh didn't feel like being careful.

He sauntered into the room and leaned an elbow on the counter, very near her. "Fresh-squeezed lemonade *and* homemade cinnamon rolls. Do you always go to this much trouble for your guests?"

"This isn't a lot of trouble." She picked up the rolling pin and began to roll out the dough into a wide, flat circle. "Aunt Rose always believed in homemade everything, and I believe in carrying on the tradition."

"Aunt Rose?"

"My great-aunt, actually. She ran the Cottage Rose until... until she died a few years ago."

"I'm sorry." Josh hated the flicker of sadness he saw cloud her eyes momentarily. She should be brightness and sunshine and innocence, that suited her more. "She must have been very special to you."

A soft smile crept to her lips. "She raised me from the time I was six. Here on Folly. Right in this house."

He heard the wistfulness in her voice, realized how much the cottage must mean to her as well. He wanted to ask more, such as what had happened to her parents, but suspected that now was not the time. Lindsay piqued his curiosity in more ways than one.

"Is that how the Cottage Rose came by its name? I thought it might be for the climber roses growing up the sides of it."

He'd noticed them during his enforced backyard R and R, a pink profusion against the gray, weathered, shingle-covered cottage. A lovely sight. Almost as lovely as the bloom on Lindsay's cheeks. The smudge of flour still rested there, and he longed to brush it away with his fingertips, but he didn't trust himself to do so at the moment.

"It was named for the roses, but I like to think it was for Aunt Rose. It suits her memory." Lindsay picked up the fresh cinnamon she'd grated and liberally sprinkled it over the flattened dough, then rolled it up like a jelly roll. She'd begun to relax around him, enjoyed sharing a little of her life with him, but she wasn't at all sure that was wise.

She lived in semi-isolation here on the island—at least as far as male company was concerned. Very few men came to the inn without a wife in tow—and here she was falling for the first one who did.

"Are you hungry?" she asked, risking a glance up at him. "These are for breakfast, but I have plenty."

Was...he...hungry? She was an innocent, Josh thought, or she wouldn't have asked in those words. She meant the rolls, but something far different came to his mind, such as the taste of her full, ripe lips, a taunting few inches away.

He couldn't resist. "You have a smudge of flour right—" he brushed his fingers against her cheek "—here."

Her hand came up and cupped over his, and Josh was sure his heart had gone into a dangerous rhythm—and not from any purported heart condition. Lindsay had an effect on him, one that he wasn't sure how to deal with. She was different from any woman he'd ever known, more fragile, more radiant, more real—and a damned deal sexier.

She laughed, a soft, bubbly sound. "I must look a sight," she said, taking a step back from him and reaching for a kitchen towel.

"Yes, a sight—a beautiful one."

Surprise lit her eyes for a moment; then she lowered her lashes over them. She wiped her cheek with a corner of the towel. "I... I'll get you a hot roll. Why don't you sit down?"

Josh had felt the overwhelming need to kiss her, and he wished now that he had done so, but the opportunity had passed. He let out a ragged, regretful sigh and took the seat she indicated.

The kitchen was small and cozy, filled with blue-painted cabinets and an old, oak trestle table with ladder-back chairs. Ruffled white curtains hung at the window. A large, lazy ceiling fan revolved slowly overhead, in an effort to cool the room that the oven—and Lindsay's presence—heated up.

She set a warm, gooey pastry in front of him. Josh ate hungrily. "Mmm, this is good," he proclaimed around a large bite.

"It's sort of a mainstay around the cottage—Aunt Rose's favorite recipe," she answered. Her back was to him as she placed the next batch of rolls in the oven and set the timer. Then she turned around and smiled.

It was a beautiful smile and one that never failed to hit him in the midsection, with the impact of a freight train, when he saw it.

"What was it like, growing up here on the island?" he asked. He wanted to know more about Lindsay Mills. He wanted to know *everything* about her.

Lindsay leaned against the counter and studied her guest. Was this idle conversation? Or did he really want to know? If he really wanted to know, she wasn't at all sure why. It was a life-style most mainlanders wouldn't understand.

"It was great, though I suppose, a bit solitary by mainland standards. We had to make our own fun most of the time." She thought about her painting. She'd started when she was only a child, first with daubs and blobs of color, then later form and substance, and finally—she hoped—some sort of message for whoever viewed her work. Not that many ever saw it. When she showed her work at all, it was in Folly's tiny art gallery.

"What about you?" she asked. "Did you grow up in Hyannis?" She suspected he'd grown up in an office. Working ten hours a day. Now she would bet it was closer to twenty.

Josh polished off his cinnamon roll and wiped his fingers on a paper napkin. "Boston—in a small, hardworking, ethnic neighborhood. Italian. Great pasta and clams and a get-ahead attitude."

"And have you? Gotten ahead, that is?"

Her question caused him a moment's pause. He supposed, looking back on where he'd been, he could answer yes. He and his partners had made great strides with the business. It was a success by anyone's standards. But when he looked ahead to where he intended to go, the answer wasn't so simple. On a deeper level—would he even know when he'd gotten there?

"I suppose I'd have to say I'm working at it," he replied, then frowned, irritated that she'd touched a nerve with her simple question.

Fortunately the oven timer rang, saving him from any further soul-searching queries she might have stored away in her pretty head. The fresh-baked aroma of cinnamon made the kitchen warm and inviting, a place to kick back and rest awhile.

Oh, God, if his partners could have heard that thought!

Was it the cozy environment or Lindsay that had him teetering on the verge of instant relaxation for the first time since... ever? Making him think it might be time to stop and smell a few flowers along the success track? He suspected she could be a serious threat to his goals, immediate and long range.

But what a delightful threat, his hormones sang out in response.

She picked up two pot holders and swung open the oven. A blast of warmth filled the room, but it was the sight of her bending over to pull out the tray of rolls that heated his body several notches higher than was comfortable. He couldn't tear his gaze away.

"Damn!" she swore, then the tray she was holding clattered to a precarious landing on the oven door.

He was on his feet. "What's the matter?"

"I burned myself on the edge of the blamed oven." She popped her finger into her mouth as first aid.

Hardly solid medical treatment, Josh thought, jolted by the sensuality of seeing her do that. But he quickly squelched the effect it had on him in favor of getting cold water on her injury.

"Here," he said. "Under the tap." He turned on the cold water and plunged her finger under the flow.

"I'm fine," she protested. "Really. It's nothing serious." She tried to tug her hand free from his.

"Any burn can be serious." He held on tight. He knew hers wasn't serious, but it was a good excuse to breathe in her delightful scent, to touch her satin skin. "Feel better?"

It did, Lindsay had to admit. She felt a little flustered being this close to him, if not silly for having been so careless as to burn herself in the first place. "I think it's fine now. Thanks."

"Not on your life. You can't be too careful with these things."

His face was inches away from hers, a dangerous distance. She knew she should pull away. The cold had helped, numbing the pain, but it hadn't numbed the feel of her hand in his.

He turned to glance at her. His eyes held a strange light; then his gaze slid over her face, settling for a long, breathless moment on her lips. Her mouth went dry, her tongue too thick to speak, if she could have thought of anything to say. Her knees trembled like reeds in the wind.

The dark color of his eyes deepened to near onyx. Or was it a trick of the light overhead? In the periphery of her consciousness she heard the water running, realized her finger was no longer anywhere near the flow, all thoughts of first aid forgotten as Josh bent his head and lowered his mouth to hers.

At first it was only a brush, a soft stirring, as he moved his lips across hers, tentatively, as if he were asking for permission to do what he wanted. Lindsay couldn't have denied him at that moment if her life depended on it. She wanted to sample the heat in him, the taste of him. She wanted to let the tingle run rampant through her body as every nerve ending quickened.

Her heart thudded in her chest, and her breath caught as he deepened the kiss, tasting, drinking in all of her. Oh, Lordy! If *her* heart was in this shape of affairs, what was happening to his? The thought skittered through her mind.

She should stop this now. Before she had to administer CPR, call the paramedics. It was bad enough that she let him hike up her steep staircase, now she was going to finish him off by kissing him to death.

Using all her willpower, she pulled away from him. "You...you can't do this," she spluttered.

"I can't, huh?" A smile edged the mouth that had just heated her to her toes. "I was enjoying it."

"No. You can't."

"I can't enjoy it?"

"Right." She turned and snatched up the pot holders then retrieved the tray of rolls from the oven door, sliding them onto the countertop. Fumbling in a drawer, she found a pancake turner. Jabbing it under one roll and then another, she popped them into a foil-lined container and snapped the lid.

Josh was shoved aside as she stirred around the kitchen like an automaton. "I don't suppose you're going to tell me what's wrong?" he inquired.

She hadn't wanted to bring up his heart condition, had avoided any mention of it all evening. He was sensitive about it, she knew.

She tore off to the front parlor, rooted around for a book to read, a soft-boiled mystery, easy on the heart. "Here," she said, when Josh followed behind her. She shoved the book into his hands. "Read yourself to sleep."

Then she grabbed a second book for herself. It didn't matter which one. She doubted she'd be able to concentrate on a word of print, anyway.

Not after that kiss.

Read?

She had to be kidding, Josh thought as he lay in bed, alternating between staring at the ceiling and then the four walls. He hadn't intended to kiss her, but those luscious lips had been so close, so ripe, so *tempting*.

What was a man to do?

She'd enjoyed it as much as he had, he was certain of that. He'd felt her respond, pressing her soft body against him. She'd smelled like a mixture of summer flowers and the cinnamon she'd been grating. Sweetness and spice.

Yeah, that was it.

Her breath had been warm against his face just before he kissed her, her lips an ambrosia of inviting delight.

He tossed down the book and stood up, feeling more restless than he ever had before. When he couldn't sleep, he usually worked, but at the moment that held no appeal. With a frustrated sigh he went to the window and studied the night. The dark sliver of moon cast strange shadows on the oleander bush. He sat down on the window seat, deciding he would see how many shapes his imagination could find there. It beat counting sheep.

And maybe he could forget the taste of Lindsay.

Chapter Three

Lindsay generally served breakfast until ten o'clock each morning, then her guests were on their own for the rest of the day. Her only other patron besides Josh, a Miss Moffitt, had already been down, eaten and set off for another day haunting the library and the island's small cemetery for her long-lost relatives. The elderly woman had prattled on about the thrill of genealogy research and the long-dead Moffitts, wilting Lindsay's ear and drinking up all the morning coffee.

Josh had not yet put in an appearance. Lindsay brewed a fresh pot while she listened for sounds that he was up and stirring. But she could hear nothing from the region of his room.

Had he put in as sleepless a night as she had?

His kiss had knocked her over with the force of a berserk bowling ball, but that didn't mean it had had the same effect on him. And thank goodness it hadn't. She would hate to have to explain to Doc why he'd taken a turn for the worse.

She'd just sat down at the table with a glass of juice when Josh entered the kitchen, a stack of what looked suspiciously like work in his hands.

"May I use your phone?" he asked. "I need to call some dictation into my office." He spread out a half dozen pages on the small desk beneath the wall phone and picked up the receiver.

Lindsay frowned at the papers.

"Don't worry, I'll make it collect," he added at her annoyed glance.

"I'm not worried about the charges, just the *purpose* of the call."

"Purpose? Oh, you mean because it's work. I, uh, just have a few loose ends I need to tie up, then it's off to relaxationville. Scout's honor."

Scout's honor, indeed. She wasn't born yesterday.

"Is that fresh coffee?" He poured himself a cup, took a gulp, then hurried to the phone and dialed. "Collect, like I said," he added with a wave of his hand meant to reassure her.

Lindsay gave a frustrated groan and stood up. "Would you like me to leave?" she asked.

"No need." He tossed the words over his shoulder, tapping his pen in a frenzied beat against the desk while he waited for the call to go through.

She snatched up her empty juice glass along with Miss Moffitt's coffee cup. Dumping both in the sink, she frowned out the window at the summer sunshine dappling through the trees, wishing she had her quiet life back. She was not his keeper. He was a grown man who was perfectly capable of looking after himself, she decided. She couldn't play gestapo twenty-four hours a day.

"What do you mean, my secretary won't take my call, Operator! Why the hell not?" Josh's voice barked into the phone.

Lindsay never eavesdropped on a guest, but this intrigued her. She turned around, rested one hip against the sink and crossed her arms over her chest.

Josh raked a hand through his hair. He could picture Eloise at her desk, shoulders squared like a battle general. She wouldn't give an inch.

Well, he'd see about that.

He hung up the phone with a stress-relieving expletive, dug in his wallet for his calling card, punched in a stream of numbers, then took another gulp of coffee.

"Eloise," he boomed when she answered. "This is your boss speaking." He had her now. "If you value your next paycheck you'll—" Josh stopped. "What do you mean you've been instructed not to talk to me?"

He'd put in the worst sleepless night of his life. The memory of the sweet taste of Lindsay's lips had him tossing and turning and staring at the damned oleander bush until the sun came up, before he finally drifted off for a few winks. Now his wily partners had blockaded his phone calls to the office.

How was he going to get any work done on this foolish vacation?

"Eloise, listen closely," he tried again. "These so-called friends of mine have set me up. They even told my charming landlady I was ready for a trip to the Coronary Care Unit and they know damned well I could pummel them to death on the racquetball court any day." That wasn't quite true. Lately he'd been putting in a lot of hours at the office with little time for exercise, but it sounded good. And if it swayed Eloise over to his side...

"They've isolated me on an island with no fax machine and yesterday's newspapers. Have a little sympathy. Take this dictation. I need letters sent to—"

Click.

"Damn!"

Josh stared into a dead receiver. He hung up the phone, plotting to veto her next raise when the matter came up.

"Interesting conversation."

Josh spun around. In his irritation he'd forgotten Lindsay was in the room. She was staring at him strangely. "You really don't have a heart condition, do you?" Her voice was low, soft...injured.

"That's right, I don't." He wasn't quite sure that was true at the moment. She looked so damned sexy with that hint of a pout on her lips, his heart had tripped into a pathological rhythm.

"You tried to tell me that yesterday when you checked in, but I didn't believe you."

The heat of embarrassment tinged her cheeks. The high color only made her more beautiful. He wondered if she knew that.

"Your partner Mr. Bainbridge said... I mean, his letter sounded so convincing that I... It wasn't true at all. I feel like a fool."

Josh vowed to get his pals for this, duping Lindsay in an effort to win their bet. She'd cared, actually worried about him, about his heart, and that was something that touched him. Deeply.

"Lindsay, I'm sorry for the deception. It was a practical joke that got out of hand. It was targeted at me, not you. You had no way of knowing what those skunks in my office were up to. Believe me, they can be very convincing when they want to be. Ask Eloise." He waved a hand toward the phone, but Lindsay had turned away from him toward the sink.

"I should have known when you weren't pushing eighty and needing a wheelchair," she said, scrubbing at a coffee cup in the soapy water. "I even gave up my bedroom to you so you wouldn't have stairs to climb."

"Hey, young guys have bad hearts, too, you know," he said to mollify her. "And giving up your room was a thoughtful gesture. I'll let you have it back. I'll move my things upstairs and yours down today."

She dropped the cup back in the sink and turned around, wiping her hands on her pink shorts that fit her a tad too enticingly for his comfort. "How hard did you try to set the record straight, Mr. Young and Healthy? You went right along with this little misunderstanding, as I recall. Lying in that hammock out back, soaking up my sunshine and my misguided concern for you, even trying to convince me your doctor wanted you to get a *little* exercise each day."

Josh wasn't quite sure that was exactly what he'd said, but he wasn't totally blameless in the matter, he knew. He raised his hands in defense. "I admit I did give in and go along with the misconception in the end, but having a pretty woman around, ready and willing to look after me, was just too tempting to refuse."

For a moment he thought that might have won her over. Her eyes widened, softening to the color of the ocean with sunlight sparkling on it, but then quickly darkened to stormy seas. "Flattery will get you nowhere with me," she said. "I'm rarely a fool a second time."

She turned back to the sink and scrubbed the hell out of the coffee cup again.

Josh jogged into town in search of fresh newspapers. He was bored, with nothing to do since Eloise wouldn't take his dictation, and he'd just lost his only friend on the island.

Lindsay.

That made him feel lower than a snake's belly. He hadn't realized how much he liked seeing the sunlight that danced in her eyes, how much he loved to hear her laugh, see her smile at him with that wide, beautiful mouth, until he'd fallen into her disfavor.

It was going to be a long, gloomy two weeks on the island now for sure. But he wasn't ready to admit defeat, admit to his partners that he couldn't do it, that he couldn't stick it out for the required time. He wanted to win the bet he had with them. He wanted that new office in Boston. He would survive this somehow—even if it killed him. He groaned at the incongruity of that thought, then picked up his pace.

Town, he discovered, was a block and a half long, a series of quaint storefronts along both sides of a tree-lined cobbled street. Folly had been a whaling port, bustling in an earlier century. Symbols of the island's proud history were everywhere. Whales—some spouting, some not—decorated signs and shop fronts. Harpoons hung over doorways. But Josh was interested in one thing—financial news from the mainland.

He jaunted down the street as if in search of gold. A weathered wooden Indian stood outside a tobacco shop that looked promising. He passed the figure and peered in the store's front window. Aha! A full rack of magazines, periodicals and newspapers lined one wall.

"Thanks, big guy," he said, patting the Indian's shoulder, then headed inside.

He found the *Times*—yesterday's. The *Globe*—dated yesterday, too. He cursed his partners who'd banished him here to languish in isolation.

"You get the financial journals?" he asked the proprietor, who looked as weathered as his Indian outside. Probably an old sailing man, Josh deduced.

"They come in on the three o'clock ferry. Newspapers, too—if we're lucky," the man answered.

"Great," Josh ground out. Now what was he to do until three?

A sense of rising panic gripped him as the whole day loomed ahead with nothing for him to do but smell the ocean breeze and watch shore birds search for mussels.

He wasn't exactly on Lindsay's favorite list, so he couldn't occupy himself with her. Much as he'd like to. Jamming his hands into his pockets, he headed out the door.

Several tourists milled about a shop front two doors down. Others were eating in an outdoor courtyard. He turned left and headed toward the wharf.

The pier was deserted at the moment. It was an hour before the morning ferry docked. Then, he imagined, the place hummed with activity. He watched the whitecaps roll in, hoping the rhythmic lapping of waves against the pilings would work some kind of therapy on his restlessness.

Withdrawal. He was going through definite withdrawal.

He found a small restaurant and had an early lunch, then spent some time browsing in shop windows, but found little to occupy his attention. Then a painting in a small gallery window caught his eye. Sand dunes, the sun setting behind them, the sky a brilliant shade of peach. There was a vibrancy to the work.

His gaze dropped to the artist's name stenciled in gold letters on a placard below the picture.

It was Lindsay's work.

Curious, he entered the gallery. Several smaller pieces of her art dotted the walls, all showing a great deal of talent. Beautiful talent.

She'd captured the island in fragile moments when the sun and sky mingled with the sea and the sand to give off its most radiant colors. It was easy to see this was a place she loved, magnified in her talent.

He stopped before a picture of a wizened old sea captain, the only portrait in the collection. It was almost as if the man were speaking through Lindsay's work, telling of the perils he'd endured at sea.

"Interesting piece, isn't it," a voice murmured beside him.

Josh turned to see the gallery attendant smiling in understanding. She adjusted her glasses and peered at the picture, then back at him. "The artist lives here on the island, but I'm afraid I can't persuade her to sell a single painting. I'm fortunate she occasionally allows me to show her work."

Josh smiled. "The lady apparently prefers to hide her light under a bushel," he said. "And that's too bad."

"Mmm," the woman mused. "It is."

Josh thanked her for letting him enjoy the paintings.

He jogged back to the Cottage Rose, breathing in fresh salt air, letting the summer sun warm his skin. There was a lot he didn't know about Lindsay Mills, facets of her that begged to be explored.

Lindsay was busy checking in guests when he arrived back at the cottage. She looked all businesslike in her task, yet tantalizingly provocative at the same time. Her slim white skirt molded to her hips and her pink ruffled blouse displayed her creamy neck and a bit of shoulder. The desire to run his lips over the delicate, exposed skin had him sucking in a breath to steady himself.

"Oh, hello." She glanced up, catching him standing in the doorway, his feelings no doubt naked on his face. She gave him a long, studied gaze then turned to the older couple loaded down with enough suitcases to stay the summer. "This is Mr. Josh Alexander, another guest at the Cottage Rose," she said to them.

The man stepped forward, his face sunburned, a flowered shirt that would be more appropriate for the tropics popping open across his wide girth. He stuck out his hand. "I'm Henry Potter and this is the missus, Stella."

Josh shook hands with them both. "You just arrive this morning?" he asked.

"Sure did. Came over on the morning ferry," Potter answered.

Josh eyed the bulging tote bag slung over the man's shoulder. "You, uh, wouldn't happen to have any newspapers from the mainland in there, would you? I'd pay five bucks for one with today's date." It was the offer of a desperate man. He might even go ten.

"Five bucks, huh?" Mr. Potter's bushy gray brows rose an inch. "I got a magazine." He dug inside the tote and extracted a dog-eared, slick copy and handed it over. "*Bird-Watchers Monthly*, real interesting," he said. "Tells all the places you can find the Pine Warbler. You do any bird-watching?"

"No, sir, I don't," Josh answered. And he'd be damned if he'd take it up—even if total boredom set in. He returned the magazine to Potter. "Thanks, anyway. I was hoping for the *Wall Street Journal*."

"Never read the thing myself," the man answered.

Lindsay did her level best to hide an emerging grin at the glum look on Josh's face, but it was no worse than he deserved. She suspected he'd gone into town searching for newspapers, and when he didn't find any, he'd tried to hit Mr. Potter up for one. Addicted. The man was positively addicted to work.

No wonder his partners had sent him here. She only wished they'd told her the truth instead of concocting a trumped-up heart condition for him, making her look the fool for believing it.

Folly was a lost outpost when it came to financial news, news of any kind. The islanders didn't care whether they heard today or next week. Good news kept, bad news they didn't particularly want to hear, anyway. But the island was a great place to unwind, which was what Josh needed to do.

Badly.

She could guide him along that path, as she did for a lot of her guests, offering suggestions, even playing tour guide on occasions when she wasn't too busy with her other duties. But when she looked at Josh, she wasn't sure playing tour guide to him was a good idea. His body had already taken on a bronzed tan, the stressful lines in his face beginning to fade, making him more devastating than ever to her senses.

She glanced away from his lean and muscular frame and back at the Potters. Then a possibility shaped itself into a viable solution.

"Henry and Stella are taking a get-acquainted tour of the island this afternoon. I recommend it to all my first-time guests. Perhaps you'd like to join them." She picked up a glossy brochure advertising the time and specifics of one of the island's guided bus tours and handed it to Josh.

He did not look at all pleased with her suggestion. "You recommend it, do you?"

"Yes..."

He handed the pamphlet back to her without even glancing at it. The corners of his all-too-sexy mouth edged up. "I think I'll wait for the *personal* tour," he said.

At three o'clock Josh jogged back into town, eager to get to the tobacco shop. This time he found what he was looking for. He snatched up a copy of the *Journal* and of every East Coast paper that had come in on the boat.

With a contented sigh he headed toward the outdoor café and settled into a chair. He ordered iced tea, then blocked out the chatter from the tourists around him and read voraciously.

The market seemed stable, almost dull in fact, he decided, poring over the stock reportings. Maybe he *could* take a day or two to relax. After all, what could he do stuck in this out-of-the-way place, cut off from the rest of the world?

Lindsay immediately came to mind.

He wouldn't mind spending some time with her.

A whole lot of time.

But he wasn't sure how to get the woman alone. She'd been busy outlining activities with the Potters when he'd left. Josh had slipped out the door before Henry could suggest he join them. He intended to keep a safe distance from the couple, not wanting them to snare him into any bird-watching expedition.

He snapped his paper open to a new page and continued to read. He was lost again in figures, thirty minutes later, when a slender shadow fell across him, blocking the sunlight on a column of percentage points.

He turned and glanced up.

Lindsay, her arms laden with several packages, stood over him, the frown of an avenging angel on her pretty face.

"Aha! I see you managed to find the financial papers after all," she said, eyeing the journal he had his nose buried in. "I thought you were supposed to be on vacation."

He loved to watch her eyes spark when she was angry. The green in them predominated over the blue, a fiery hue that revealed the depth of her passion within. But he decided to keep that observation to himself. She was riled enough.

"I don't suppose you'd believe this is relaxing?" he asked halfheartedly.

"You're right, I wouldn't."

He folded his newspaper into a lumpy square. "Then what do you suggest?"

"I suggested it earlier."

"The tour with the Potters? It's too late—I saw the bus whiz past here twenty minutes ago."

"Oh."

Her mouth looked so delightful framing that word, he'd like to make her say it again. He'd love to hear her say it when he made love to her, he thought, his mind slipping into a territory it shouldn't. Lindsay, with her sweet ways, her innocence, could be a definite threat to life as he'd come to know it.

He should remember that.

Last night he'd played hell getting to sleep in that room, knowing that it was hers, knowing that she'd slept in that bed, the moonlight slanting across her soft body. It had him tossing and turning and wondering what it was she dreamed about as she slept. Did the night frighten her? Did she remember a man's kiss? Or dream of a clear morning to capture some elusive seascape.

Tonight he'd move his things up to the top floor, let her have her own bed again. Then, at least, maybe *she* could sleep.

"Join me," he suggested to her when he saw the waiter approaching the table. He stood and pulled out a chair for her, then reached for her packages, but she held on to them.

"I have errands to finish. And *you* need to throw away that stack of newspapers and do some sightseeing."

She turned on her heel and set off with the sassiest little walk he'd ever seen. He dug in his shorts pocket for money, tipped the waiter, grabbed up his reading material and hurried after that delightful swing.

She suggested sight-seeing, and Lindsay was the only sight he cared to see. "Mind if I tag along?" he asked with his best lady-killer smile.

Chapter Four

Lindsay turned and saw him fall into step beside her. She wished he wouldn't smile at her that way. It did crazy things to her breathing.

"You won't find my shopping very interesting, I'm afraid," she said as she headed into Arno's Pharmacy. She picked up a wicker shopping basket. "Wouldn't you rather take a tour or try out the beach?"

He followed along behind her. She knew he was restless. He was a man used to being busy, superbusy, no doubt.

He was feeling cut off from the rest of the world by those few miles of water that separated Folly from the mainland; isolated from work, fresh newspapers, stock market reports, everything that was important to him. She wasn't sure why that bothered her as much as it did, but she couldn't deny a certain sense of disappointment.

"The tour bus left, remember?" he reminded her. "And the beach is crowded."

"Excuses." She reached for a tube of sunburn cream on the top shelf.

"I'll get it, shorty." He reached up and effortlessly plucked a tube from its resting place.

"Just watch who you're calling shorty." She frowned at him. "And I need three tubes. I like to keep them on hand in case my guests overindulge in the sun."

"Do you always think of everything?" He reached for two more and dropped them into the basket on her arm.

"I try to."

She started walking down the aisle. Josh followed along behind, thinking maybe the beach might not be a bad idea—if she'd rub some of that cream on him. He watched her sashay through the rows, picking up one item and then another as she went.

He could really get into this sight-seeing stuff. A satisfied grin edged his lips.

"Stocking up for this year's batch of guests, are you, Lindsay?" the pharmacist asked, when a few minutes later she was ready to check out.

"'Fraid so, Mr. Arno."

The man's face lit like an overdecorated Christmas tree when Lindsay followed that with a smile. Josh couldn't blame the guy. She had the same effect on him, maybe worse.

Lindsay introduced him, and Arno stuck out his big hand.

"Josh came over from the mainland for a little R and R," she said, then turned to Josh to see him frown.

"Well, you came to the right place for that," Arno chuckled richly. "There's not much to do around here *except* relax."

"I'm finding that out," Josh said with a low grumble. He reached for Lindsay's packages.

"You take care now, Lindsay. And good luck to you, fella," the man added.

Luck. He would need it if he was going to make it through this vacation. Lindsay was his only hope of survival. He stuck to her like a shadow as they walked on. "What's the next stop on our list?" he asked.

Lindsay arched an eyebrow at him. "*Our* list?"

"Just a manner of speaking."

She swallowed a groan, then entered the fragrance shop where she found the special little scented soaps she put in the guest bathrooms, stocked up on candles in case Folly's sensitive electrical system failed again and picked up another package of potpourri that always reminded her of the flowers on the island's moors.

At the spice store she bought more fresh cinnamon for the breakfast rolls, then pronounced that she was done.

"That's it?" Josh asked. He put the package of potpourri he'd been sniffing back into the sack.

Lindsay had to smile at the frank look of disappointment on his face. He really didn't know what to do with himself.

Why had she ever agreed to be the man's keeper?

They were silent for a while as they walked along the bricked sidewalk. The sun was beginning to angle its way down behind the dunes. A light salty breeze blew in from the ocean. It played with the ends of Josh's hair and toyed with his shirt collar. She settled her gaze on something less dangerous to her senses than the man beside her—Thompson's sign over the hardware store. Much safer.

Not safer, she realized a moment later. They were nearing the gallery where her artwork stood in the front window for all to see. Showing her paintings was still difficult for her, and she suspected it always would be. Nina had pressed to let the gallery show her work, and she'd only agreed because she'd been able to catch the island in certain magical moments and she wanted others to love its beauty as she did.

As she feared, Josh drew her to a stop in front of the place. "I have the perfect wall for this in my office," he said quietly. Too quietly. "But the gallery owner tells me the artist won't sell any of her art."

He reached for her hand, his fingertips lightly touching hers, but the easy grasp felt like a stranglehold.

"Josh..."

"Your work is beautiful, Lindsay." His voice was a vibrating whisper on the afternoon air.

She didn't know what to say. Praise embarrassed her, and she wished he wouldn't look at her that way, his dark eyes gleaming, a small smile hovering at the edges of his lips. "It's...it's something I do for enjoyment. I can't...I *don't* want to sell any of them."

"You love the island very much. It shows in your work."

"I paint what I see. I try to capture the essence of the island, its heart."

"You're the one with the heart, Lindsay. As big as all outdoors. Giving of yourself to the guests, everything from special scented soaps and pretty-smelling dead flowers—"

She laughed. "That's potpourri and they're not dead, they're dried."

"Whatever. You know what I mean. You're a giver, Lindsay. A nurturer. To your soul."

They'd walked on, leaving the gallery window behind. That hadn't been as bad as she'd feared. Josh had seen something in her work, had seen what she'd tried to do. That pleased her. He hadn't let go of her fingers, but slid his hand fully around them. It had happened so easily—like his kiss the night before. She hadn't done a thing to stop it. And she didn't do a thing to stop this, however much she knew she should.

Josh would be going back to the mainland soon. She belonged here. Would always belong here. She needed to remember that.

* * *

Lindsay looked up to see Josh standing outside her bedroom door, his suitcase in his hands. "I'm moving in," he said.

Her eyes widened in surprise. The man worked fast, she thought for one mad moment. But she knew what he meant by his loaded statement. He wanted to give her back her own room.

"I'll pack up your things and move them down," he said, settling his suitcase inside the doorway and looking around at the small room she'd taken.

"That's a thoughtful offer, Josh, but not necessary. I'm fine here, and the other room is larger and more comfortable."

"And *you* need to be downstairs where you can help your guests if they need you."

That was the main drawback, she knew. She was more inaccessible to her patrons being on the top floor.

"This room is fine for me," he said. He sat on the bed and tested it with a bounce up and down, as if already taking over the place. The old springs creaked under his body weight; then he paced across the floor and peered through the window. "It even has an ocean view."

Lindsay sighed. "But wouldn't you be more comfortable—"

"No. I want this room. Let's get your stuff packed up."

Let's. The man seemed addicted to using the plural when referring to things she considered hers alone. No way was she going to allow him to handle her personal belongings. She already felt exposed to him.

He was learning everything about her all too rapidly. He'd seen her paintings, peered straight into her soul at what she'd tried to accomplish with them. He'd kissed her, dragging emotions and needs to the surface, needs she didn't know what she would do about once bared and vulnerable. Just the light curl of his fingers around hers this afternoon had her feeling like a silly schoolgirl in love.

Not something she should be feeling with a summertime guest, a mainlander.

"I can pack up my own things," she said more sharply than she intended. She dragged the boxes she'd unpacked only the day before from the back of the closet. "I don't have that much, really."

"I can do *something.*" He followed her into the closet, swept up the hanging clothes and folded them over his arm. "I'll take these downstairs and be right back."

The man was impossible, she thought as he left. She sighed and pulled open a drawer.

He was back in minutes, taking the stairs two at a time, catching her with a stack of lacy underthings in her arms. She stuffed them into a small suitcase and turned for the last items, but she wasn't quick enough.

Josh stood beside her, a tumble of lacy silk falling over his large male hands. "Mmm, what's this?" He lifted a melon-pink teddy for closer inspection; then his wicked gaze fell on her, taking in her slender frame with a slow, lingering sweep and an equally slow grin.

Her stomach muscles tightened reflexively. She stared at the frilly thing for a moment as if she'd never seen it before, then snatched it off his index finger and wadded it into the suitcase.

When she turned around again, he had a white lacy bra dangling from the same finger.

"Do you mind?" She snagged it away from him.

"Mind what?" he asked and searched the drawer for more.

"Out," she ordered. "Out, out, out. I'll finish up here."

"I was only trying to help."

"Help like yours, I don't need." She pointed the way to the door. This time he went, but not before hefting the box of her painting supplies on his right shoulder. "Holler if you need me."

Fat chance. Lindsay stared after him. She was ready to wish that imaginary heart condition on him, that way she might not be so tempted to strangle him.

Annoyed with him or not, she couldn't deny her growing attraction for the man. Everything he said or did, every expression on his too-gorgeous face had her all but panting after him.

It was ridiculous, that's what it was. Maybe she'd been isolated on the island too long. But her one brief foray to the mainland was not an experience she cared to repeat.

She'd spent two years in Boston, studying art, but the innocent life she'd led here on Folly hadn't prepared her for the mainland men she'd met.

One man in particular. Brant. With her trusting ways, she'd fallen in love with him. Or at least thought she had. Brant had been charming, attentive, good-looking—maybe not as great looking as Josh, but handsome by any female's standards. And capable of breaking a woman's heart.

It had taken her several years to put Brant and her failed relationship with him into perspective. She had been nothing but a diversion for him, naive and different from other women he'd dated.

Had she been more the sophisticate, had she grown up in the city with her mother instead of on Folly with her beloved Aunt Rose, she might have been more prepared for the men out there in the real world.

Josh was a man from the real world, and he'd be going back to that world in less than two weeks. He had goals and plans that were different from those of her own. She knew that, yet she enjoyed his kiss, his touch, even his teasing, far more than she should. Her head told her not to be a little fool again, but she feared her heart wasn't doing a whole lot of listening.

She slammed one drawer, then checked the next and the next for any leftover pieces of intimate apparel that Josh might taunt her with later, but found nothing. She checked the closet and under the bed to be sure she'd collected all her personal things. She had. The sheets had been put on fresh this morning, as with all the guest rooms.

She straightened the small area rug, then, satisfied she'd made the room as ready as she could, she shifted one box into her arms and picked up the suitcase. The other box she would let Josh get. It was filled with innocuous enough things. Unless he had a fetish for women's shoes, she thought, glancing at the three pairs sticking out the top.

That night, after he'd settled into his new room on the third floor, Josh went in search of Lindsay, the Monopoly game he'd found in the bookcase in the front parlor tucked under his arm. Henry Potter had kept her cornered in conversation half the evening. So had another guest, a woman named Moffitt, who had a strange penchant for snooping through cemeteries.

He found Lindsay reading in a small sitting room, hidden away off the kitchen, yet close enough to the pulse of the Cottage Rose that she could keep an eye on her patrons should they need her. He hoped that tonight none of them did because he wanted her all to himself.

She glanced up from her book.

"Care for a game of Monopoly?" he asked.

For a moment he thought she might say no, perhaps order him out in no uncertain terms as she had upstairs when he'd tried to help her pack up those sexy little undies of hers. He hadn't known such a tiny sprite of a woman could pack such a wallop of a temper. But, instead, she smiled. "Monopoly, huh?" One silken eyebrow raised. "Do you cheat?"

He splayed a hand across his chest as if mortally wounded. "Cheat? Me?"

"I'll take that as a no." She cleared away a clutter of magazines from the low coffee table in front of her and tossed two overstuffed pillows to the floor, then settled onto one of them.

Josh took the other, trying to hide his elation at the fact that the evening was shaping up nicely. Lindsay had changed into white jeans and a stretchy blue top that would drive him out of his mind if he didn't find something else to divert his attention.

Money. He counted out the game board's money with unwarranted deliberation. "You want to be the car or the cannon?" he asked with a lazy smile. There might be something to this relaxing thing, he decided, settling in for an enterprising game.

"I'll be the—" she pursed her lips as she looked over the selection "—the hat." She picked up the small silver game piece resembling a man's top hat and set it on Go.

Josh dropped the cannon beside it, certain that one more pucker of those luscious lips of hers and he'd be in real trouble. Snatching up the dice, he shook them hard. "I hope Potter doesn't disturb us. Has he gone off to bed already?"

Lindsay smiled over at him. "He and Stella turned in early. They want to be off before sunup to scout out some rare species of marsh wren," she explained.

"Ah, yes, the one with a purple head or was it a dotted yellow beak? He tried to inveigle me into going along. Said I was missing a rare opportunity."

She laughed, a sound that had Josh wanting to hear it again. "And what excuse did you give him?" she asked.

"I suggested he take Miss Moffitt along, that I'd secretly found out the woman could warble every mating call in the bird kingdom."

"You didn't?"

"I'm sure he'll be after me once he finds out it isn't true." Josh tried to concentrate on the game in front of him and less on how Lindsay's shirt made her eyes look more blue than green tonight. Chameleon eyes, he thought. They changed, depending on what she wore, depending on her mood. Tonight her mood was soft, warm... inviting. Too inviting.

He threw the dice and tripped around the board, buying up property along the way. Lindsay went to jail. The practical side of her kept her from paying the fine and bailing herself out, he realized. Meantime he bought Park Place and Boardwalk.

It didn't take long before he had two and three hotels on every prime piece of real estate and most of the game's money in his coffers. Lindsay's funds had dwindled to a few paltry dollars. Even the bank was running low.

He rubbed his hands together in sweet glee as Lindsay's playing piece sat primed for yet another sojourn through his pricey neighborhood.

Lindsay shook the dice an unnecessary number of times and considered her chances of making it past Josh's property. They were slim to none. Somewhere along the way she'd lost control of the game—though she doubted she'd ever had it. Maybe if she'd been less aware of the man seated across from her, concentrating more on his playing strategy instead of his entrancing smile and the way his hair curled over his shirt collar, she wouldn't be in this pickle.

And what had happened to fun? What had happened to relaxing? This was supposed to be an innocent little game, a game between friends.

"Throw the dice," Josh urged restlessly.

"Keep your shirt on," she grumbled back, then wished she hadn't said that. It brought a fresh image to her wayward thought processes—Josh, minus that knit shirt clinging to his muscled torso like peel on a mango.

"Correct me if I'm wrong," she said as sweetly as her bad mood would permit, "but I thought the purpose of this game was enjoyment. You know, *fun.*"

He acted as if those little red blocks of wood were truly hotels, complete with paying guests and hot and cold running water. He hadn't smiled since he'd bought his first piece of property. His brow was furled into a Wall Street frown deeper than the Grand Canyon. His shoulders were hunched forward, his eyes steely beads, lacking the least bit of compassion.

He was just waiting for her to land on his precious Boardwalk, which was a definite possibility.

"The purpose of this game is to *win*," he returned.

She frowned back at him. "That's very important to you, isn't it—winning?" Sadly she realized that it was. Very possibly it was his entire purpose in life. It was a wonder he *didn't* have a heart problem. Or at least an ulcer.

She was about to tell him that, when he turned to her and offered a placating grin. "I'm doing it again, aren't I? I'm supposed to be relaxing, right? And I'm not."

"No,. you're not."

He toyed with his stack of five-hundred-dollar bills, every one in the game except for the single one she had stashed beneath the board in front of her for safekeeping. She supposed that, too, was a clue to the differences between them.

"One more game," he said. "This one strictly for fun. I promise."

That, she suspected, was a promise he wouldn't be able to keep for long. She didn't want to play, not this game, not with him. She leaned forward, her elbows on the coffee table. "Tell me," she asked, "why is winning so important to you?"

She didn't know what kind of answer she expected, offhand or some soul-wrenching confession, but whichever, she wanted to hear it, had to hear it.

He shrugged, sending his wide shoulders up, then down. Lindsay silently cursed herself for watching the action, enjoying it.

"I'm competitive. It's my nature. I suppose it comes from being pitted against my brothers from the time we were kids together. All we knew was besting each other, playing to win it all, the whole enchilada. I don't apologize for it...it helped make my business the success it is, it made me an achiever, a doer. And—" he paused and let his gaze caress Lindsay's face "—it got me sent here for rehabilitation. That can't be all bad, now can it?"

Lindsay wasn't so sure about that, she wasn't sure about anything at the moment, except that this man could make her heart flutter like a bird caught in a fisherman's net.

She gathered up the game, spread out across the coffee table. Josh helped her. "Did you really grow up with a gang of brothers?" she asked him.

Perhaps it was curiosity that made her want to know more about him, about what made him tick. Perhaps it was something more.

"A gang? We were practically a football team. There were six of us," Josh said proudly. "And we were close. You picked a fight with one, you got us all."

Lindsay was certain she wouldn't want to tangle with any of the Alexander boys. "And did they all turn out to be...overachievers like you?"

"I suppose you might say that. There are two doctors, one attorney, a company executive and...a rocket scientist."

Her eyes widened. "You're kidding."

"Only about the rocket scientist. He's really a helicopter pilot." He laughed. "The black sheep in the family. And what about you? You said you were raised by your aunt. No brothers or sisters?"

"None," she answered. Her childhood was another difference she and Josh shared. She'd grown up a solitary child—solitary, but not lonely. Aunt Rose had made the best playmate a little girl could have. Lindsay still treasured the memories.

She'd missed her parents terribly when she'd first come to stay with Aunt Rose, but the woman had eased the sense of loss that could have been devastating—her father's death in the awful car accident, her mother's need to work that took her from Lindsay in yet another way, to the mainland.

Her mother had never liked the island, not like Lindsay did, not like Lindsay's father had. Her mother seemed to be driven by a force Lindsay wasn't sure she understood or would ever understand. She was proud of her mother. She had gone to work for an auction house in Boston, working hard, traveling the country, even Europe, buying up estates, antiques. Now the company was hers, but she worked even harder.

Lindsay occasionally got her to come to Folly to get away from the mad pace she set for herself, but she could never stay long. She found the island too confining.

Because Josh was looking at her far too intently for comfort, Lindsay set the lid back on the Monopoly box and laid the game aside. She would put it back in the bookcase later. The game had been revealing in vital ways, exposing them to each other more and more.

Then Josh stood up and paced the room that she tried to keep as her private living quarters, though she'd never actually declared it off-limits to her guests. "I noticed that you don't have any of your paintings hung about. Except for one." He paused before the large seascape of the windward side of the island.

Lindsay stood up. "I didn't do that painting," she answered, hugging her arms to herself. "My father did. It... it's the only one I have of his."

Josh turned and studied her. "Then he's an artist, too."

"Was. He was killed in an accident when I was six."

He hadn't asked her about her parents. Now he realized her father's death coincided with when she'd come to live with her aunt. Had both her parents died? He wanted to ask more, but something fragile in her look held him back. At certain moments there was a waiflike quality to Lindsay and at other times—like when she'd ordered him out of her room—she could be tough. Strangely both sides of her intrigued him. "I didn't know about your father. I'm sorry," he said.

She shook her head and smiled. "It was a long time ago."

"Your work is very similar, you know—except... I don't know, this painting has a more earthy beauty to it somehow, as if your father captured the island's rougher edges. This *is* Folly, isn't it?"

She nodded. "It was a special spot of his. I've tried to paint it myself, but I never quite get it right."

"I'd like to go there to see it."

"Perhaps I'll take you," she said.

Josh felt as if she'd promised him the moon, full of cream cheese, and her along with it. He crossed the room to where she stood. The dim lighting gave her eyes a dusky glow. Her lips looked soft and inviting, beckoning him like a siren's song. He bent his head, brushing their fullness, stealing their sweetness.

He wanted to stretch the moment into forever, but knew he dared not. Lindsay was far too tempting, his emotions on far too shaky ground. Reluctantly he drew away, stroking a finger across those soft lips he'd kissed.

"G'night, Lindsay."

Chapter Five

Lindsay was hosting a full table of guests at breakfast the next morning. Josh had come downstairs about ten o'clock and consumed his first cup of coffee. The Potters and Miss Moffitt had returned from their morning of bird-watching and decided to have seconds on Lindsay's cinnamon rolls to tide them over until their next meal.

Her other two groups of guests, the Liebermanns and the McGowans, who'd checked in the day before, had gotten the same late start on their morning that Josh had, but they'd quickly eaten and run, eager for their day of sight-seeing.

That left her with the motley crew of bird-watchers—and Josh—none of whom looked like they had any intention of going anywhere anytime soon.

Lindsay had hoped she could clear away the breakfast dishes and get on with her work schedule, but with a frustrated sigh, she poured a cup of coffee for herself and resignedly settled into the empty chair beside Miss Moffitt.

"You'll simply have to come with us tomorrow, Joshua," Stella Potter chattered away to Josh, seated on her right. "Tell him, Henry, tell him what we saw today. You simply won't believe it...a purple-breasted waterthrush," she went on, detailing what she'd just asked Henry to relate.

Lindsay glanced at Josh over the rim of her cup. Their eyes met, his beleaguered gaze locking with her amused one. He took a quick gulp of coffee and turned back to Stella. "Is that right? I didn't know there were any of those left in this part of the world."

Somehow he'd managed to make his voice sound conversational instead of bored, but that only encouraged the group. Henry gave a census report on the bird, while Miss Moffitt enthused over what a wonderful new hobby she'd found. She loved it, though she admitted she was still a little wet behind the wings at it.

Lindsay wondered if that meant she intended to give up her genealogical treks through cemeteries, but didn't dare ask for fear of being drawn into the conversation.

She'd much prefer to sit here and observe Josh's misery—although she wasn't sure being anywhere within twenty feet of the man was safe. Not after last night and that small, quiet kiss of his that had sent her senses reeling.

How could such a minuscule moment in time cause such a lasting devastation? she wondered. She'd spent the better part of the night trying to forget it had happened, but one small glance at his sexy mouth this morning and she knew she'd forgotten nothing about the feel of it.

She wished he would go off sight-seeing somewhere, anywhere—study footprints in the sand or search for wild berries or look at passing ships—anything but soak up her coffee and her kitchen space.

"Hawklets? White-ruffed hawklets? You saw three of them?" she heard Josh say with forced enthusiasm in reply to Henry and Stella's ongoing prattle.

"And their parents," Henry added. "They nest on the cliffs, you know, in among the crags." He leaned back, looking enthralled at having a captive audience. "This particular species is growing more and more extinct. Stella and I wrote our congressman about it. Terrible. Just terrible if they should die off."

"The hawks or the congressmen?" Josh asked.

Henry guffawed. "Definitely the hawks. It almost happened to the peregrine falcon, you know. And then there was the brown pelican. Now there's an ugly bird." He shook his balding head. "But...one of God's creatures, and you just can't let 'em die out."

Josh shot Lindsay a plea for help that bordered on the desperate. She knew he was bored out of his skin. He was a man used to discussing high finance with influential clients all day long and he'd been reduced to talking baby birds with Henry.

She almost felt sorry for him, almost, but not quite.

There were any number of relaxing activities he could be doing on the island instead of sitting here, listening to a conversation about the demise of the hawk, but so far he'd resisted every one of them.

Last night's Monopoly game could not be termed a relaxation experience. Not for a man like Josh. A corporate raider would have played the game with less ardor.

Still, she knew she had to break up this little morning coffee klatch if she was going to get any work done. Time was wasting. And Josh's restlessness had deteriorated to the spoon-tapping stage, a frenzied beat against her plaid tablecloth, a definite clue to his inner turmoil.

She cleared her throat, calling the table to attention.

All eyes turned to her.

"It's such a beautiful day outside, you need to go and enjoy it. How about a trip to see the cranberry bogs?" she proposed, mustering the right degree of excitement into her voice. She felt like the activities director on a cruise ship.

Make that the Titanic, she amended as she chanced a glance at Josh. He didn't look at all pleased with her tour suggestion. Well, it would be perfect for her older guests. She would have to come up with something else for Josh.

Something on the *far* side of the island, preferably.

She needed to keep a healthy distance from the man if she was going to maintain her perspective. He might kiss great, but she didn't intend to become his summer dalliance, help him fill in his hours of forced idleness, ease his boredom.

"That sounds like an interesting tour," Stella exclaimed. "What do you think, Henry?"

Lindsay soon had the group shuffled out the front door. Everyone but Josh, that is. She heaved a sigh and turned around in the front entry hall to find him standing next to her, so close she could see the tiny razor nick on his jaw and the intent glitter in his dark eyes. "It looks like it's just you and me," he said. "I'm ready for my personal tour."

His voice slid over her like a warm ocean breeze, nearly shattering her resolve. "I never promised any... personal tour." She hoped he didn't notice the quaver in her reply. His very presence taunted her with the memory of the feel of his lips, warm and sensual and... "If you wanted to see the island, you should have gone with the others," she reminded. "Henry would have liked having another man along."

Josh grimaced. "Henry's a very nice man, I'm sure, but I hardly want to spend any more of this vacation with him than an occasional greeting at breakfast. Now you, on the other hand—"

"Are busy." She crossed her arms over her chest, standing her ground.

"Is that any way to treat a guest?" One dark eyebrow raised in a mocking salute, and a smile edged up at the corners of his mouth. "You paid more attention to me when you thought I was sick."

"That's because I mistakenly believed you needed special, uh, consideration."

"I do."

"Not *my* consideration. You're perfectly able-bodied." Her gaze slid down the able frame in question before she caught it somewhere below his knees. She dragged it back up to his face and frowned at the smug way his smile had deepened. "You don't need my help," she finished lamely.

"Oh, but I do."

"Sure. Like I need a case of the measles. The ten-day variety." She stalked to the desk, picked up a goodly supply of brochures and shoved them into his midsection. "This should keep you occupied for a few days. Now if you'll excuse me, I have work to do."

"Damn," Josh cursed aloud as he watched his only hope of a tolerable day retreat down the hallway. He sank back against the desk and frowned after her. He'd suffered through Henry and Stella's bird chatter and endured the sight of Lindsay, looking sexy and sweet at the far end of the table, until he ached inside—all in the hopes he could spend some time with her.

Doing what, he didn't know.

Or care.

She was the most enticing thing this island had to offer, but she'd just blown him out of the water.

He raked a hand through his hair. "Damn," he cursed again, then glanced up as Lindsay walked through with a load of bedding in her arms.

She offered him a smile and a tiny wave, her fingers waggling at him from under the stack of sheets. "Have a nice day," she said before starting up the staircase.

Have a nice day! Doing what? Watching the grass grow? He shoved off from the desk and made his way to the kitchen for a glass of lemonade, then a trip to the backyard so he could lie in the hammock and observe the little marks the stringed contraption made on his bare legs.

Every man's idea of a fun day, he thought, shoving through the screen door a few moments later. He maneuvered his body into the hammock, something he was getting all too proficient at lately, and stared absently up at the sky.

What was so damned intriguing about Lindsay Mills, anyway? he asked himself, taking a swig of lemonade. Okay, she was pretty—but then, so were a lot of other women he'd dated. He ticked off a few names on his fingers, thinking of their attributes, trying to pinpoint the difference.

Melanie had great legs, long and gorgeous, but somehow they couldn't hold a candle to the trim, tanned pair Lindsay sported. Jennifer. Hmm. Scratch her—he hadn't seen her since... forever. In fact, he hadn't seen Melanie in a while, either.

But that was because he'd been busy lately. Working long hours. Now he'd been forced into this isolation on an island where there was little else to do but while away hours and hours in nothing activities.

If he were back on the mainland, there were any number of things he could be accomplishing. A long list of them paraded through his idle mind, work that was now maddeningly out of his reach. He felt hamstrung, put out of action. His body tensed with the sheer frustration of it.

He'd left copious memos for Eloise. Even more for his partners, things that had to be handled while he was away. But Eloise still refused his calls. And his partners had probably closed the office doors and gone sailing.

That last thought set anxiety astir in him anew. He took a huge gulp of lemonade as a sheen of sweat broke out on his forehead.

Damn! It wasn't fair being cut off from the world, from the things he needed to stay on top of. He stared up at the trees. Relax, he chided himself. The market was quiet. This was the perfect time for a vacation—if there was such a thing as a perfect time.

But that was yesterday, the market had been quiet *yesterday.* Anything could have happened since then. He knew how quickly things changed in this business. So did his partners, but they'd ushered him off to Siberia—well, a summer version of Siberia. Folly.

He felt his heart begin to chug inside like a locomotive trying to top a hill. His chest tautened. Indigestion. He'd gulped the damned lemonade and now he had indigestion. He never got indigestion.

It was because he'd been forced into taking this vacation. He was never sick at work, never missed a day at the office in his life. He passed a hand over his forehead. The sweat there had turned clammy. Maybe he was getting the flu. That was it, the summer flu.

He sank back in the hammock, trying to find a comfortable position. There wasn't any. The more he tried to relax, the tighter his chest felt. If he didn't know better, he'd think a three hundred pound gorilla was using his ribs for an accordion.

He lurched to a sitting position, causing the hammock to sway crazily. Dizzy. Now he could add dizziness to his growing list of ailments. He felt like hell.

He was sick—*really* sick.

A frustrated groan escaped his lips at the irony of it.

Lindsay had managed to get the beds made with no more than an occasional peek through the gauzy curtains at the man in her backyard hammock. She'd been unable to resist the draw of the sight of him, stretched out in sexy repose. But at last peek, she noticed he seemed to be growing uncomfortable with the fine art of relaxing—something she doubted he would ever be able to perfect.

She chanced one more cursory glance down from the second-floor window, a final glimpse at the man who could make her heart flutter in a ridiculous patter. Just to check up on him, she assured herself. Just to be certain he was doing what he was supposed to be doing. Taking life easy—or at least attempting to.

But this time the hammock was empty. His lemonade glass lay forgotten in the grass beside it. She gave a small shrug. He must have gone for a walk or maybe a jog along the beach, she decided, letting the edges of the curtain fall together.

Putting her distracting guest out of her mind, she gathered up the dirty linen, carried it to the old laundry chute in the hallway and sent it on its way to the basement. The wooden chute groaned and creaked, but like every sound in the centuries-old house, it was music to Lindsay's ears. She loved every noisy board, every squeaky door, even though at times the place seemed to be falling down around her ears, a repair or a new remodeling task all too frequently looming on her horizon.

Like the fading wallpaper in the upstairs hallway. She gave it a studied once-over. This winter, if she could find a pattern she liked at a price she could afford, this project had to take priority.

With a sigh she started for the stairs, only to stop on the top step. Josh sat on the bottom one, a shoulder propped against the wall, looking like he'd just lost his last friend.

She trod down the stairs cautiously, curious as to why he was sitting there, doing absolutely nothing. Obviously he had not gone for a walk—or a jog. Her brow furrowed. Why had he deserted the hammock to take up residence at the bottom of her staircase? What was he up to?

The third stair creaked as her toe touched it, announcing her presence. He turned around and gave her a weak smile.

Even though it wasn't his usual hundred-watt variety, it still had an effect on her. She edged closer, eyeing him with measured suspicion. "What are you doing here?" she asked. "The tobacco shop fresh out of the financial papers?"

"Very funny!"

"Then what?"

He fixed her with a somewhat baleful glance. "I don't... feel well," he said.

So that was what he was up to! She descended the rest of the stairs and stood in front of him, nailing him with her best I-don't-believe-it-for-a-minute smile. "That old chestnut isn't going to work with me, Josh Alexander. I'm seldom a fool a second time, so you can forget this little ruse of yours. It isn't going to get you any more attention from me than I give my other guests."

He frowned glumly. "I don't expect you to believe it. Just help me up the stairs. Does that doctor friend of yours make house calls?"

"House calls!" Oh, brother, he was really pulling out all the stops. She *ought* to call Doc Tobias just to show this man up for the fake he was!

"Are you going to help me or not?" He gave a petulant growl.

"Not a very convincing act," she said as he wobbled to a standing position in front of her. His face was sheened with perspiration—he'd probably run in place in the front parlor to work up a sweat or maybe it was water he'd splashed on himself, courtesy of her kitchen faucet. Whatever the cause, the effect was a dampened T-shirt that hugged his well-shaped pecs.

"Never mind the stairs," he said, elbowing past her to flop onto Aunt Rose's old fainting couch in the front parlor. "I'll just rest here until Doc arrives."

Fainting couches were not designed for men, she decided, observing the way he dwarfed the blue damask piece. Even in his half-sitting position his legs hung over the end of it. He kicked off one tennis shoe, then the other and pressed a hand to his chest.

"Not going to die with your boots on?" she asked archly.

Josh raised up on one elbow to glower back at her. Enough was enough! "You're going to be sorry when you find out I'm really sick," he informed her, but that didn't do a thing to wipe the smile off her smirky mouth. He groaned and flopped back against the cramped couch, wishing he didn't have that niggling little fear that all this might be his heart—for real this time.

And Lindsay wasn't about to believe him.

He might lie here and die before he could convince her he was telling the truth. But wasn't it his fault—at least in part—for duping her the first time? Now when he needed—really needed—a little of her TLC, he would play hell getting it.

In truth, he was beginning to feel a little better. He'd taken a few deep breaths, forced himself not to panic, to relax, think pleasant, soothing thoughts, and it had helped some, but he still wasn't ready to run a foot race. Not even against a turtle with a game leg.

No—if he was going to save himself, he'd have to do it on his own. "Give me Doc's number," he barked. "I'll call him myself."

Or the paramedics, if the island had any, he thought as he tried to stand and was hit by a fresh wave of dizziness. He promised himself that if he lived through this, he'd see a doctor for a physical at least occasionally. No more putting it off, no more excuses that he was too busy.

"I'll call Doc," Lindsay said, seeing Josh's face blanch with the exertion. She couldn't think of any way the man could fake sudden pallor. But if he was, if it was all some trick of his, a ruse to get her to look after his deceitfully ill body, she'd make him wish he were sick—or worse!

"Don't put yourself out," he snapped, but she ignored his sarcasm and eased him back down on the couch.

"You rest easy," she said, stuffing a blue paisley pillow behind his head. "I'll be right back."

She gave him one last, wary glance to reassure herself this wasn't some ingeniously planned fakery before going to the phone.

He really didn't look at all good, and that worried her as she waited for Doc to answer.

Lindsay paced the hallway, waiting for Doc Tobias to finish his exam. He'd arrived in short order, his well-worn black bag in hand. After a quick initial evaluation he'd moved his patient to Lindsay's first-floor bedroom for more privacy and an in-depth going over. He'd said nothing, only an occasional "Aha" or "Hmm," which Lindsay couldn't interpret, but had surmised as bad.

What if Josh had to go to the hospital, Folly's little twelve-bed facility? Or be flown to the mainland for more intensive treatment? If anything happened to him, she'd never forgive herself.

She stuck an ear to the door and listened unabashedly for sounds of conversation, anything, but could hear nothing. What was taking so long?

She'd just resumed her pacing when the bedroom door opened and Doc's silver-white head emerged through the opening. His kindly, round face was unreadable, but she was certain hers wasn't.

"Come in, Lindsay," he said solemnly.

With trepidation, Lindsay obeyed.

Josh stood beside the bed—should he be standing?—his tanned, muscled body bare to the waist. She allowed her gaze to ripple over his shoulders, his chest, the dark curls that furred like velvet down his flat, firm abdomen, disappearing into his low-slung cutoffs.

This did not look like a man who, a few moments before, was pale as a ghost and dizzy when he stood. This man looked healthy enough to tackle the Olympics.

Or to make love.

"You did the right thing in calling me," Doc said, which brought Lindsay back to reality and her heart up into her throat.

Oh, Lord, she thought. Appearances were deceiving. She squeezed her eyes shut. Josh was sick, really sick. "How...how bad is it?" She didn't want to hear Doc's answer, but she had to know.

"He had the symptoms of a heart attack, but in this case it was a false alarm."

"False alarm?"

"It's an interesting syndrome that can happen when a fast-track person tries to relax. Sometimes they have the real thing, but Josh was lucky."

"Lucky?"

Doc nodded sagely. "I'm going to run him by the hospital for an electrocardiogram, of course, but I think the test will bear me out. Josh went from a pace that would kill a lesser man to total inactivity. That put an undue amount of stress on his system."

Lindsay's eyes widened in shock. And she'd forced him into that hammock to do absolutely nothing but stare at the sky overhead. It could have killed him—it almost had!

She glanced at Josh who was wriggling into his T-shirt beside Doc. He tucked the long ends of it into the snugness of his cutoffs, then sat down on Lindsay's bed to pull on his tennis shoes.

"I've outlined a regimen of exercise and relaxation for him while he's here on Folly," Doc went on. "A little of both will do him a world of good. He needs to decompress—like an astronaut coming out of orbit, so to speak. Just not all in one dose."

"I see," Lindsay said quietly. Doc wouldn't have had to share any of this with her, but she was glad that he had. As angry as Josh could make her at times, as much as she tried to deny the growing attraction she felt for her summer guest, she had to admit that she cared about him. And what happened to him.

Very much.

Josh glanced up from tying his shoelaces to catch Lindsay's gaze on him, a warm, caressing gaze that stunned him even as it kicked him in the libido and sent his heart rate soaring back up to that dangerous rate Doc's stethoscope had found moments before.

She cared, actually cared, about his unworthy hide, although he was certain that if questioned about it, she'd deny it vehemently.

He tucked that little bit of knowledge away for further use, not certain what he intended to do about it.

He knew he should run like hell and as fast as he could. What did he need with a relationship, a *serious* relationship, in his life? For he had no doubt that Lindsay would be, could be, nothing less than serious to him. She was not a casual woman. She would be there for a man—always.

A forever kind of woman. The kind he'd always wanted.

Someday.

When he was ready.

Doc turned to him. "Good. You're dressed. We'll go by the hospital and get that test now. And on the way we're going to have a little talk about that lifestyle you lead back on the mainland."

Josh had the feeling life was a-changing for him.

And not just in the way Doc was threatening.

Chapter Six

Over the next few days Josh got all the attention from his lovely landlady that he could handle—it just wasn't the kind he wanted.

He was struggling, really struggling, to do what Doc Tobias told him he had to do. Moderate exercise linked with moderate amounts of rest. He had no problem with the moderate exercise. He got up in the mornings before it was even daylight and jogged five miles along the beach. He felt great, renewed, revitalized in a way he hadn't felt in a long time.

Afternoons he'd formulated a group of calisthenic and aerobic-type exercises for himself. But he wasn't sure he could handle the *rest* part. Doc had told him in no uncertain terms just what his road-to-success life-style would do to him if he didn't change his ways.

He knew the man was probably right—okay, he *was* right—but he'd always thrived on the thrill of competition, of winning, of succeeding. It was part of him. He wasn't sure he could spend time in noncompetitive activities for long.

Lindsay had outlined a long list of them for him to try, everything from meditating to developing a relaxing hobby like the sort the Potters enjoyed. Birdwatching was not for him, he'd told her. And the meditating always ended up in a sensual parade of tantalizing images of Lindsay that had his hormones in a constant state of overload.

He needed to get his mind back on stock portfolios or the Japanese bond market and keep it there. But she'd caught him with a copy of *International Investor* tucked inside the *Field and Stream* that she'd borrowed from Doc for him to read.

Today promised to be better, however. Today Lindsay had agreed to join him on a bike tour of the island. She had a terrific little ten-speed tucked away in a shed behind the Cottage Rose. Josh jogged into town and rented one for himself. He even picked up a picnic lunch for them from The Crow's Nest.

Lindsay was ready by the time he got back. She looked like one of those fantasies he'd been meditating on, dressed in temptingly abbreviated white shorts and a pink halter top. She'd tucked her long blond hair up under a pink baseball cap that had Folly monogrammed across the bill. Pink whales dangled from her earlobes, doing a perky dance with every turn of her head.

"Ready?" he asked.

Lindsay was certain she would be sorry she'd agreed to this bike tour, but she still had guilt feelings for not believing Josh when he'd really been ill. She also felt responsible for him. At least she preferred to think of it in those terms, rather than the real reason—she cared about him.

He'd been trying very hard to follow Doc's advice, and she wanted to do what she could to help.

"Ready," she answered. "What's in the box?"

"Our lunch."

"Lunch? But I thought we'd be back by then."

"I want to see *all* the island and I figure that will take us the whole day."

Lindsay groaned. What had she expected from a man who did nothing by degrees? "Then I'm going to need sunscreen," she said and pulled a bottle out from the pouch she'd attached to the back of her bike.

Josh watched with desperation as she smeared the white lotion over her lush legs, stroking in long, upward motions that nearly had him coming unglued. He swallowed hard and pulled out a map of the island to divert his attention.

"Want some?"

Her soft voice coming at him nearly knocked him off his bicycle seat. He glanced up from the route he was mentally mapping out for them and looked into her guileless blue-green eyes.

"Sunscreen. You really should put some on. At least your nose."

Josh stared at the bottle in her hands. "Maybe later," he said and kicked up his bike stand.

Lindsay shrugged and tucked the bottle away. "I think we should take the beach road and head west," she said when he started off in the other direction.

"Why?"

"That way we pull the hill first while we're still fresh, then it's downhill on the way back."

That was smart thinking, he supposed. And he could use the challenge of a hill to get his mind off Lindsay. He turned his bike around, following her lead.

Riding behind her was hazardous to his peace of mind, he decided as he watched her rounded bottom move rhythmically up and down on the bike seat with each pump of her pedals. He looked his fill for a slow moment more, then with a low groan, pulled up alongside her where the view was of the road ahead. A slight but steady incline. To his right lay the ocean, aquamarine in color today, nearly matching the hue of Lindsay's eyes. To his left, small cottages faced out to sea.

As they rode farther, gentle moors replaced the cottages, but the ocean stayed everpresent in their view. He breathed in deeply, taking in its scent.

Maybe Doc had something. He was beginning to feel great. "I see why you love it here on the island," he said.

She turned to glance at him, her face flushed from the ride and the warm sun overhead. Josh wasn't sure he'd ever seen a woman look more beautiful.

Or more tempting.

"Sometimes I think I'm the richest person on earth," she admitted with a smile, as if sharing her most secret confidence with him.

He understood what she meant.

"How do you feel?" she asked. "Any chest pain?"

"Hey, Doc gave me a clean bill of health—remember?"

"Just checking."

She pumped the bike faster, cresting the hill. Josh followed suit; then they coasted down the other side, letting the wind blow away every care.

The coastline was becoming rockier, less sandy. They passed the airport. Had it only been a few days since he'd jetted in here on that small commuter plane? Today, possibly for the first time in recent memory, he hadn't thought about work. And it hadn't sent him into traumatic shock.

But that was because his mind was on something else. Lindsay. Today he had her all to himself. Finally. After days of scheming to get her away from Henry and the other guests, away from her duties of running the Cottage Rose, away from her reluctance to spend time with him.

He hadn't kissed her since that night they'd played Monopoly—and he ached to do so. He'd tried to forget the memory of the taste of her mouth, the soft invitation of it, but he couldn't.

When the sun reached its peak overhead, they wheeled into a shady spot under an old struggling locust tree where the waves lapped lazily at the shoreline.

"I'm starved," Lindsay proclaimed. "What did you bring?"

"I think the Crow's Nest called it their lover's picnic," he said with a flourish of the chilled wine bottle and two flutes he'd suggested be added to the basket of goodies.

That brought a blush to Lindsay's face that didn't come from the exertion of their ride. "Oh," she said, then matted down a stand of beach grass for them to sit on and pulled the basket between them.

As protection? From him?

But given his mood at the moment, perhaps she needed to protect herself. He'd never been with a more sensual woman than the one he was with right now. It was a sensuality she didn't have to work at, it was just part of her. Innocently part of her.

And that made it all the more dangerous.

Lindsay set out the picnic lunch Josh had brought along, busying herself with the activity to keep her mind off the devastating man beside her. They were not lovers. Far from it. Josh was a summer guest, nothing more, but for one moment his words slid over her with the warm possibility of it.

What would it be like to let him make love to her, slow, bone-wilting love, the kind that lasted until the sun came up in the morning? To watch his eyes darken with passion? To lose herself in that hard, lean, unyielding body?

She was certain the reality of it would far outstrip the fantasies that had her tossing and turning the past few nights. "It seems you thought of everything," she said as Josh poured a glass of wine and handed it to her.

The wine put the lunch they were sharing into a more intimate category, and she didn't need any push in that direction. Each moment they were together seemed intimate somehow—even when they were surrounded by other guests—as if she and Josh were the only two people in the world, in the universe.

"I think this private moment in the most beautiful spot on earth deserves a toast," he said, raising his glass.

She smiled at his appreciation of nature's beauty, pleased that the world of finance in which he lived and thrived hadn't destroyed that capability in him and that this was something they could share.

"Yes, a special toast... To the island," she said, her glass—and her gaze—meeting his.

"Not to the island—to the woman I found there," he insisted, his voice as hypnotic as the sound of the waves that lapped a few feet from them.

She didn't know how to respond to that. Heat threaded through her, a heat she wasn't sure was caused entirely by the wine. Unsettled, she set her glass aside and picked up a fat deli sandwich, an *unintimate* deli sandwich, and took a bite.

Somehow she needed to get this day on a more platonic footing. But with Josh looking sexy and all male a few inches away, platonic would be difficult at best. She marshaled her gaze on the scenery dead ahead—the blue ocean, a few lazy terns wheeling overhead, a sprinkling of marshmallow clouds. A safer view than the one of Josh in a pair of well-worn tennis shorts and a faded black tank top that left far too much of his bare, bronzed chest exposed for her sanity.

"This is the western-most tip of the island," she said, throwing out the dry fact as if it were of vital importance. "There's a small mileage marker on the end of that jetty that claims the mainland is twenty-two miles straight ahead."

Josh glanced in the direction of the stone jetty that pierced through the waves, then to the distant horizon for a lengthy moment. Hyannis was over there. His home. A brief seagull's flight away—if he were a seagull.

"So near and yet so far," he said, half to himself.

"What?" Lindsay turned toward him, her ballcap askew, a few wayward strands of her blond hair escaping down her neck and in front of her ears. She reminded him of a moppet, but an incredibly sexy moppet.

"Nothing. I was just thinking out loud," he replied, but he wondered how he could pursue a woman who so obviously belonged *here* when he needed to be *there*.

With a disgruntled sigh he reached for another sandwich and bit into it. He wasn't sure he could get Lindsay out of his system, but he didn't doubt that it would behoove him to do so.

He'd carefully mapped out his life, and it didn't include involving himself in a relationship that would divide his time between his work and trips to Folly. No, when his time here was up, when he'd won his bet and returned home victorious, he needed to get on with his plan to open that new base of operations in Boston.

"This is a great place to see the sunset," he heard Lindsay say, her words breaking into his thoughts. "I come here sometimes just to sit and watch it. It slips down into the water in the most gorgeous fiery colors."

Damn, Josh thought. With one simple mention of a sunset, she had him forgetting his life plan, his precious timetable for success. She had him wanting to watch that sunset with her.

"If you're through eating, we'd better get moving," he said a bit more sharply than he intended.

There was a look of surprise on her face when she turned to him. Josh packed up the hamper, not daring to glance her way. He wanted to toss the picnic stuff aside, take her in his arms and kiss her, not just once, but again and again. He wanted to laze the day away with her, watching sunsets, sunrises, rolling surfs. He wanted to make love to her here in the soft marsh grass until they were both beyond sated.

"You're right," she said. "We need to get going if we're going to see the whole island."

"I don't think this is what Doc Tobias meant by exercise," Lindsay huffed a few hours later.

Josh had insisted on exploring every road on the island to its conclusion. The trip around Folly, if they stayed to the main road circling the outer circumference, was fifteen miles. Lindsay was certain they'd logged twice that and they still had a ways to go.

Her legs ached and her face felt windburned. She wanted to rest, make that *collapse*, preferably in the closest bathtub of hot water.

Josh seemed to have just hit his stride. The sun had bronzed his arms and legs. He'd worked up a sweat that sheened on his strong, muscled shoulders and beaded on his face and chest. His dark hair curled damply over his forehead.

He looked like a magnificent athlete about to win the decathalon, while Lindsay was certain she merely looked bedraggled. She blew upward on her bangs that hung in her eyes. "You've managed to turn a simple outing into a marathon event, and I, for one, want to rest."

Or die.

If she could muster the strength for it.

Braking her bike to a snap of a stop, she crawled off its frame, not caring if Josh rode on and got himself hopelessly lost on some rarely traveled dune road and was never heard from again.

Josh stopped, too, then wheeled over to where she stood, wiping the back of her hand across her sweat-stained face.

"Here," he said, whipping out his water bottle and handing it to her. "Take a drink. You look like you need it."

That confirmed her bedraggled theory.

She took the bottle, taking note of the look of apology on his face. It wasn't enough. He'd nearly killed them both from the exerting ride. She'd never before considered herself a pantywaist, but this had been the trip from hell.

She took a long, slow sip and resisted the urge to pour the remainder of the bottle over her face and down her halter top to cool off. She didn't need the front of her wet, her nipples puckering themselves against the fabric for Josh's enjoyment—although that would probably take his mind off her unkempt appearance.

"Thanks," she said, handing back the bottle. "Care to join me on that big, flat rock over there and rest until this time tomorrow?" She didn't wait for his answer but started off in that direction.

"I really am sorry," he said, following. "I just get carried away when I get into something."

Lindsay could well imagine why his partners sent him here. They had to, so they could catch their collective breaths. They probably had high hopes he wouldn't return.

She never got into anything that avidly, not even her artwork. That was something she enjoyed; painting calmed her, enriched her, soothed her. She never made it a marathon event. Maybe she lacked passion, she didn't know.

Her mother ran her antique business with that kind of drive, as if the devil himself were after her. She seldom relaxed, seldom did anything just for the enjoyment of it. It hurt Lindsay when she would call and cancel a visit to the island because she'd found out about a major estate sale in Chicago or California that she just couldn't miss out on.

It had hurt worse when Lindsay was a child and had banked all her hopes on those rare, special visits.

She'd vowed then and there that when she was a mother her children would be her consuming desire, not her painting, not anything else. Her children would have a mother *and* a father in full attendance.

"At least I was doing something relaxing," Josh defended as Lindsay collapsed onto the rock. He sat down beside her.

"Oh, *relaxing*—is that what you call it?" She pulled off her pink cap and fanned herself with its bill. Her hair tucked up under it spilled to her shoulders. She lifted it off her neck and fanned herself there, too.

Feeling half a degree cooler, she twisted her hair up under the cap again.

"Leave it down."

"What?" She turned to him sharply.

"Your hair. I want to see it down." He reached out a hand and lifted the ballcap off her head, loosening the tresses once more. "Beautiful. Like bright sunshine," he murmured, letting the strands glisten through his fingers. "*You're* beautiful, Lindsay."

He hadn't meant to kiss her, but he found himself doing just that. And she was returning that kiss in a way that would inflame any man alive, her soft lips tempting him shamelessly, moving beneath his with a slow heat.

Her hair teased the backs of his hands as he cupped her face. He slid his fingers outward, tangling them in its silkiness, drawing her to him, drawing her deeper into the kiss. Her body heat swirled around him, her soft scent driving him close to madness. A velvet-throated purr slipped from her lips. He heard his own deep groan of agony.

God, but he was on fire. On fire with wanting her.

In the distance he heard the pounding of the surf, nearly as deafening as the force of his heartbeat. His tongue teased at her lips, begging them to part, to admit him entrance, and when they did, his heart outdid the surf by double the decibels.

He gave a groan of need, of madness, as he sank into her sweetness, drowned in her scorching heat. He drew her closer, feeling the push of her breasts against him, that rounded shape that had driven him crazy all day.

"Lindsay..." Her name slid from him in a whisper. "What is it you do to me?"

She drew a deep, shuddering breath, and he knew she was as affected by what passed between them as he was, she was as ill-prepared to deal with it as he. She pulled back a half inch, not much in distance, but enough so they could each cool off some. He needed to or he'd be making love to her right here on this uncomfortable rock.

She reached up a hand to push aside a tendril of hair at her temple. Her fingers trembled in the action. He felt every bit as shaky. Inside. Lindsay had knocked him for the proverbial loop. With her kiss, with her touch, with her nearness. Never before had a woman hit him in the solar plexus with as much force.

"I'm not sure we should do this again, Josh." Her voice had the same tremble as her hand. "It makes me..."

He stroked a finger along the satin of her cheek. "Makes you what?" he asked when she didn't finish.

"Makes me...want you."

Josh's body, which had barely begun to cool, simmered again with a fresh heat. Lindsay's directness, her innocence, made him want, too. Want *her,* like he'd never wanted another woman. "I know," he said with a ragged sigh. He tilted her face up to his with the tip of his finger beneath her chin. "I want you, too."

They moved together, as helpless in their action as two magnets. Her arms slid around his neck, twining there with a delicate, subtle strength. His lips sought her sweetness, his tongue darting into her parted mouth with a new hunger.

He ran his hands up her sides, over the halter top. She had nothing on beneath the soft knit scrap, and his fingers traced the curve of her ribs with ease. His thumbs found the delicate underside of her breasts, stroking their fullness upward to her nipples, taut and tangible beneath the pink fabric. He sucked in a breath at the lush feel of her, then let it out on a throaty purr. He'd never known a woman so soft, so desirable as Lindsay, so capable of sending tremors through him.

Lindsay felt a dangerous heat suffuse her body as Josh's thumbs rasped over her breasts, her nipples, sending a fierce ache to the inner core of her being. Her heart thudded wildly and her breath hung suspended in her throat.

His kiss devastated her senses, his marauding tongue setting fire to them.

From some distant part of her brain she knew she had to stop this, that it was all wrong, that Josh was wrong for her. But her body ruled supreme at the moment. It sang beneath his touch, an entire chorus she didn't want to ever end.

He felt so good beneath her hands. She ran her fingers over his muscled shoulders, up the strong column of his neck. She tangled them in his hair, thick and unruly from his ride in the wind. She pressed her breasts more fully into his hands, wantonly, needfully, thrilling to his caress.

Their thighs touched, bare, fevered skin to bare, fevered skin. The crisp, dark hairs on his leg prickled against her. Her senses had never been so keenly alert, so finely tuned to every sensation. He smelled like the tang of the sea mixed with his own very male scent, a scent that surrounded her.

She knew that every moment she prolonged this, she came dangerously closer to being unable to stop, closer to fracturing her heart. Josh was a dream, a fantasy who'd come to share her island with her. For a while, a brief moment out of time. But he didn't belong here. He had a life beyond Folly, beyond *her*.

The roar of the surf, present in the distance, rooted her to reality, to where she was. On the island. She ran her opened palms over his shoulders, feeling the flesh-and-blood man beneath them, an attempt to make him real, too, to make her aware of who and what he was. A man who was here with her, alive, breathing, making her revel in his kiss, the feel of his hands on her, but every bit a fantasy that would disappear like smoke in a few weeks.

With every ounce of willpower she could muster, she broke the kiss and drew back from the heat of Josh's body. She felt the tease of the wind that fluttered between them, separating them like a barrier.

"Lindsay..."

Her heart squeezed at his soft whisper of her name, but this had to end. Here. Now.

She shook her head to clear her senses, then stood and walked on shaky legs toward the shoreline. This was the windward side of the island and the beach was rocky, the surf angry. It had always drawn her with a fascination. Even in its fury it calmed her somehow, but not this time. This time it offered her nothing, except maybe a sense of loss.

Josh drew a hand through his hair, his eyes on Lindsay standing beside the ocean and hugging her arms to herself as if the sun overhead had suddenly turned cold. She looked so small, so fragile beside the pounding surf. He wanted to go to her, needed to go to her. All he could think about was the salty taste of her lips, the feel of her in his arms, her soft breasts in his hands. He dragged in a deep breath, then exhaled slowly, raggedly.

He wished Lindsay didn't mean so much to him, but she did. That smile, so dangerously childlike, yet ever so womanly, undid him like none had before. Her laughter, her sunshine, warmed a part of him he hadn't known needed any warming. He loved her sweet caring, even her scoldings.

He started toward her. He didn't want to get involved in a relationship with Lindsay, yet he couldn't seem to get enough of her.

She turned to him as he approached, then glanced away again. They needed to sort out a few things—their feelings, for starters. He looped an arm around her shoulder, not like a lover, yet... very much like one. "Lindsay, we can't deny this attraction between us."

"Yes, we can."

The simplicity of her statement made his mouth twitch at the corners. "I don't think so. It's there and it's real. It isn't going away."

She didn't answer him, but he felt her shoulders coil with tension. She hugged her arms tighter around her as if to shut him out, shut out the truth of his words.

"You propose to just ignore it then?"

"There's nothing to ignore."

Like hell there isn't, lady. "Are you trying to tell me you didn't feel anything back there on that rock a few minutes ago?"

She remained stubbornly silent, stubbornly still, stubbornly wrapped into herself. He wanted to shake her.

"That, uh, kiss didn't mean a thing? Or the way I held you? The way *you* held me?" Damn, but his skin was still on fire from the touch of her sweet hands moving over him.

"We...we had a wonderful day together. Can't...can't we just leave it at that?"

A wonderful day together. Yes, it had been. Lindsay had made it wonderful. But leave it at that? Forget one minute of it? He could easier fly. "Okay, Lindsay, we'll play it your way. We'll live under the same roof, see each other every morning, every night. We'll smile at each other, brush past each other in the hallway, and we'll pretend there's nothing between us." He turned her to him, tilted her chin up and gave her a kiss, long and deep and stirring. Then he pulled away and smiled into her glazed eyes. "We'll forget it all."

Chapter Seven

"Damn the man's hide—his beautifully tanned, healthy, gorgeous hide," Lindsay muttered as she stared across the gentle heave of the dunes, then at the blank canvas in front of her. She waved her paintbrush in the air as if she hoped it might attract inspiration.

She'd spent three miserable days trying to ignore Josh's presence in the large house, but she'd run into him around every corner. She didn't want to admit that he might be right, they couldn't ignore each other and the attraction that cropped up between them every time they came within ten feet of each other. Make that twenty feet. No, twenty miles.

She suspected all the distance in the world wouldn't help. Even here on the dunes, where she usually found such peace, the memories of his kiss, the feel of his body, that know-it-all, sensual smile of his heated the blood in her veins.

Each morning he would show up at breakfast, looking better and better. Each night he'd smile and tell her to sleep well, as if he intended to have no problem in that department. He'd even stop her in the middle of her day's work and ask directions to the tennis courts or the dive shop or the kite rental.

There had to be some way to get the man out of her system.

She studied the blue of the sky overhead and attempted to match the color from her palette. She would stay here all day if she had to, until she got it right. Josh was not going to ruin her afternoon. He was not going to intrude on her creativity. This was her world, where she was in her element.

Just because she was attracted to him didn't mean she had to give in to that attraction. She had other things to do with her life. And right now one of those things was to paint this picture. She wanted to enjoy her afternoon escape from the Cottage Rose—and Josh's all-pervading presence there.

Why did she have to be so *aware* of the man, keenly aware of every move he made? The way he stroked his jaw when he was thinking about something? The way his mouth quirked up more on the right than it did on the left when he was amused? The way the laughter lit his dark eyes when he laughed outright?

She didn't need Josh in her life. She was content. She had her island. And she had the Cottage Rose to run.

Her brush flew over the canvas in bold, sweeping strokes, her irritation fueling each swath, her pent-up emotions transferring themselves to the picture. She didn't care that the painting would be all wrong—as wrong as Josh was for her.

She should be painting the far side of the island, capturing the riotous surf, the jagged shore—that would better fit her mood. She had hoped that painting the muted sea and quiet dunes would calm her, but so far it hadn't helped.

She took a step back and studied her creation. It was different—not altogether bad—just not her usual style.

It had more color, more... more...

Passion?

No, not *passion*. She refused to consider the word that had just slipped out, and tried to think of another to define what was there on the canvas.

Fervor? Intensity? Spirit?

Her word search drew to an abrupt end as she glanced up and saw Josh jogging toward her across the dune... *her* dune... where she'd come for peace and quiet. He was clad in faded black jogging shorts, his feet tucked into a derelict pair of running shoes. His chest was bare, and the sunlight caught and glistened on his sweat-sheened muscles.

Her artist's eye couldn't help but admire the beauty in his long, graceful stride, couldn't help but size up exactly how she would paint him if he were her subject. But he wasn't her subject, he was her... annoyance.

Did the summer sun have to make him this bronze, this sleek? Did he have to exude such vitality, such sexuality, that she itched to take brush in hand and capture him on canvas?

She tried to concentrate on some flaw in him, some lack, something that turned her off. But she suspected that if she stared all day, she wouldn't find a single thing. "Don't tell me—you were out for a jog and just happened to be in the neighborhood," she taunted as he loped up beside her and aggravatingly tried to inspect her painting over her shoulder.

He didn't even have the decency to be winded from that sprint up from the beach.

"Something like that," he purred. "I saw someone wielding a paintbrush with a vengeance and figured it had to be you."

"I was not wielding my brush with a vengeance." She turned toward him, with her back to her work, hoping her body would shield it from his scrutinous gaze. It wasn't her best effort, but even if it was, she didn't want him to see it.

Her turn, however, brought her nose to nose with him, or rather, nose to that bared chest of his. She swallowed hard and resisted the urge to comb her fingers through the dark curls nestled there, sample the feel of them, the texture. She hoped the urge was merely the artist in her, but she suspected it was more.

She backed away, and in the process, angled her easel away from his prying eyes.

"The sensitive artist at work," he said with a smile she wanted to wipe off his face. He'd invaded her privacy, her space.

Well, he could just jog on by, over the next sand dune, with that gorgeous body of his. "The sensitive artist would like to get back to her work," she said, poking her brush into the madder blue on her palette, hoping he would take her broad hint and leave.

"I'm ruining your inspiration?"

Not so much ruining her inspiration as he was diverting it. Definitely diverting it. But she didn't intend to tell him that. "I just want to finish while I have the light."

He sat down a few feet away and watched while she worked. "Don't mind me, I'll be quiet as a mouse," he said. He plucked a sea oat and clamped it between his teeth.

Lindsay's own teeth clamped in frustration. She'd never been so unable to work. She stabbed a dot of madder blue onto the pristine sky, darkening it like a thunderstorm.

"Wanna go swimming later—after the light goes, that is?"

Her brush swerved drunkenly across the canvas. "Now look what you made me do."

"What?" He was on his feet in a quickened second, glancing over her shoulder.

She hadn't meant her rhetorical question as an invitation to view her painting-in-progress, but he'd taken it as such.

"I like it," he said. "Except for that smudge *ri-i-i-ght* there—" he pointed to the smear he'd caused "—it's wonderful."

It wasn't wonderful. She snatched the canvas away from his prying gaze. "Do...you...mind?"

"You know, Lindsay, you shouldn't be so sensitive about your work. In fact, I think you should have a showing. Yeah, a real show. Maybe in Boston. I have this friend who could—"

She frowned over at him. "I don't want a showing."

"But you need one, every artist needs to show his work. Just a small one to start, then—"

"Forget it." She reached to put away her paints. Her creative mood had dissipated.

"I could help you tap into that potential of yours, market yourself—"

"I don't want myself marketed, and my potential is just fine the way it is." She painted for herself, but she doubted that was something this competitive man would understand. He wouldn't be satisfied unless she outrivaled Picasso. She folded up her easel with a snap.

"You're not quitting! You've still got the light." He waved at the sky.

"I may have the light, but my peace and quiet is shattered."

"Peace and...? Oh." He gave a sheepish smile. "It's me, isn't it? I've interrupted your inspiration."

"Let's just say you didn't do it any good."

He stuffed his hands into his shorts pockets, tautening their already disturbing fit. "I suppose artists work better without an audience."

She studied his chastened features. The man was so exasperating. "It helps."

He reached for her easel and unfolded it, steadying it in an upright position. "There," he said. "You paint, and I'll just jog on back down to the beach." He set her canvas back on the easel. "You think about what I said... about having that showing—then we'll talk. Later."

Lindsay clenched her fists at her sides to keep from unleashing them on him. The guy just didn't get it. "There's nothing to think about," she retorted with determination. "I'm not going to have any showing."

He put his hands on his hips. "Lindsay, if I wasn't so concerned about interfering with inspiration, I'd kiss you right now." With that he turned and took off across the dune toward the beach.

She watched his retreating backside more avidly than she should. Finally, when he'd disappeared from her view, she turned to stare at the half-finished painting in front of her, but her muse had fled. No doubt it was cavorting on the beach, along with her traitorous good sense.

* * *

Josh smiled, pleased with himself that he'd done what he could to further the beauty of art for mankind. He'd sacrificed the taste of Lindsay's lips for the greater good. His feet barely touched the sand, his lungs filled with the fresh ocean air, he reveled in the surf's spray against his skin.

Lindsay deserved a show. She deserved to have her paintings seen by the world. And in doing so she'd also be spending time on the mainland.

With him.

Okay, so maybe he wasn't all that self-sacrificing.

Maybe he was selfish. But Lindsay brought that out in him. He wanted her all to himself.

He might even extend his vacation a week. Just a week. Wouldn't that surprise his partners!

Well, he deserved it. And one week wouldn't take that big of a bite out of his success timetable. He was really getting into this exercise routine he'd set up for himself. Besides, he wanted to spend more time with Lindsay.

Over the next few days Lindsay had managed to avoid Josh and any further conversation about a gallery showing by keeping super busy. She'd checked in two new guests, which added considerably to her workload—and to the excitement around the Cottage Rose.

The girls, Tanya and Steffie, eighteen and college-bound in the fall, were a breath of fresh air around the place. Or perhaps, more like a hurricane.

Their respective families had given them the two-week summer vacation on Folly as a graduation gift, and they'd arrived the day before, loaded down with bikinis, beach balls and blow dryers. The blow dryers had blown the inn's tender fuses three times already, but Josh came to the rescue, braving the dank basement to replace the shot fuses. The girls had gushed their effusive thanks to him on all three occasions. In fact, they carried on as if he'd slain dragons for them.

Josh had tried his male best to steer clear of them, but they didn't miss an opportunity to flirt. *Outrageously*. Between dodging the Potters and the oversexed teenagers, he was a man in misery.

Lindsay knew she should save him from their clutches, and she would—after she'd enjoyed the fun a little while longer.

"We're beaching it today—wanna join us?" Tanya cooed at him over breakfast.

Josh swallowed his orange juice, as if he had the whole orange stuck in his windpipe, as the bikini-clad duo dropped into chairs on either side of him at the table and beamed up at him adoringly. He shot Lindsay a fevered glance, begging for rescue, but she only cupped her chin in her hand and smiled back in perfect imitation of the girls' besotted gazes.

"Please say yes," Steffie echoed. "You can show us how to scuba."

Josh frowned at Lindsay, then turned to the teenagers.

"Can't today, girls," he said. "I, uh, promised Lindsay I'd see about rewiring the inn's old fuse box."

Lindsay nearly choked at his excuse. Rewiring that box would take more than a day—and more money than she had in her coffers. Instead, she'd bought up the island's entire supply of fuses, hoping it would be enough to last until the end of the girls' stay.

"The least you could have done was save me from them," Josh said when the pair had grabbed their beach towels and left.

"And you could have come up with a better excuse than rewiring my ancient electrical system," she parried back.

"Well, I could have another look at it." He gave her a dangerous smile. "If you'll hold my flashlight."

Lindsay didn't dare let herself be in the dark with him, not when just the thought of it made her hot all over. She needed to keep a tight rein on her feelings for Josh. A relationship with him would extend only as far as the shoreline and then he'd be gone, out of her life, and she'd be left with only the memory of his kisses. No, she couldn't let him affect her the way he did.

But she hadn't a single clue as to how she should put a stop to her runaway emotions. She understood why Tanya and Steffie were rhapsodic over the man. Her own hormones hummed the same melody. Chorus after chorus. She couldn't blame the girls—not when the man wore that tantalizing after-shave so early in the morning, not when he brought those sexy muscles of his to the breakfast table before the previous night's dreams had even worn off.

"I intend to update the wiring system sometime next year," she explained. "In the meantime, I'll keep replacing fuses."

"*You* will?"

She began to clear away the breakfast dishes. "I'm perfectly capable of it—unless, of course, you want to continue to impress my two, young, female guests with your electrical prowess. I'm sure *they'd* be willing to hold your flashlight."

"You wouldn't be jealous—just the teensiest bit?"

"Of course not. Why would I be jealous?" She snatched the juice glass from in front of him. "What do you intend to do today since you told those two you'd be elbow-deep in fuse boxes?"

He smiled. "Spend time with you."

"Oh, no. I'm going to be elbow-deep in the Cottage Rose's finances—juggling bills to keep the place looking like it's in the black."

"Perfect," he said enthusiastically. "Finance is my area of expertise."

What was that fragrance she wore? And why did it drive him so crazy? Josh wondered as he leaned over her, trying to keep his mind on her finances instead of her hypnotic, flowered scent. He drew in a deep breath, reveling in her femininity before forcing his distracted mind back to the figures in front of him.

He had to hand it to her: she kept neat, orderly records. But one thing was apparent, the old house ate up what little profits she made from the guests. "The place is barely in the black," he said. "What about you? Where's your salary?"

She shrugged her small shoulders and looked up from the oak rolltop where they were working. "I don't take one usually. I need to put every cent I can back into the Cottage Rose. When I took it over, it wasn't in the best shape. Aunt Rose didn't have a good head for business. And she'd let more of the repairs slide than she should have."

"Like you're doing with the electrical system."

"I intend to take care of that, but as you can see from the books, I don't have an abundance of ready cash. I was hoping that after this tourist season..." Her voice trailed off, but Josh caught her meaning.

If there was money left after the taxes, utilities, insurance, advertising—operating expenses ad nauseum—she'd tackle the wiring. Which wouldn't leave her much for a salary—even if this season was roaringly successful.

"I do most of the repair work around here myself. And I'm not too bad at it. I can fix a rusty pipe as well as any plumber."

He could picture her wielding a wrench half her size, tackling the archaic plumbing all by herself. A certain sense of admiration for her determination swept over him, but along with it came a surprisingly strong urge to protect her from all of that. To take her away with him, pamper her, love her, keep her safe from worry. But would Lindsay leave this house? Ever?

Running the Cottage Rose was important to her. Making the inn a success was equally important. She loved the place. That much was obvious from all that she did, from all of herself that she put into it.

Lindsay watched the play of emotions on Josh's face. He was used to high finances, not her small operation. She prided herself on her business acumen, which he no doubt found flawed. What else could have brought that dark scowl to his face?

She hadn't wanted him looking over her books, but he'd determinedly bullied her into showing them to him with an offer to help, an offer she didn't need or want. Not that he couldn't help her. Profit and loss was something he understood, but could he understand how much this place meant to her? How much she needed to carry on what Aunt Rose had started? How she just couldn't let the place die?

"Okay," he said. "Let's see what we can do here." He dragged a second chair up to the desk and scooted in next to her. Whether she wanted his expertise or not, she was getting it.

The tiny alcove seemed narrower than ever with Josh so close. Her figures danced on the page as she tried to keep focused on them. His leg nestled next to hers in warm intimacy. She tried to ignore the heat that curled low through her body, sapping her strength.

Think of the man as the accountant you've never been able to afford, she begged her mind. But her body remained determined to focus on skills other than his financial ones.

His hand worked her ancient adding machine, the relic clicking and thunking, filling the tiny room with its noise. He paused occasionally to drag a hand through his hair, his forehead furrowed in thought; then he punched in more numbers.

"How are your reservations running for the remainder of the season?" he asked without looking up.

"If it continues like this, I'll do all right."

His head swiveled toward her, his dark eyes narrowed on her. "Could you be a little more specific?"

She frowned over at him, then snatched a folder from a cubbyhole in the desk. Now she remembered why she preferred doing her own bookwork. Accountants—and the IRS—always wanted precise numbers.

She shuffled through a few letters requesting accommodations. "I have deposits for ten more reservations—most are two-week stays, a few are three- to four-day stays," she said, riffling through the small stack.

"That's it?"

"For now. I get referrals from some of the other places when they're full. And if I'm full, I refer my overflow to them. It works very well," she added at his doubtful look.

"If you advertised in some of the upscale magazines, you could have a hundred percent occupancy rate from the first of the season to the last week," he pointed out.

"But then I wouldn't have room for drop-ins, tourists who come over on the ferry and fall in love with the island and decide to spend a night or two."

Josh studied her for a considering moment. She wore her hair twined into a long braid again this morning, and he ached to loosen it, strand by silky strand. "Lindsay, it's always preferable to have secured income as opposed to possible income. You're running a business here, not a port in the storm."

"I still prefer word-of-mouth to paid advertising. Besides, if I run this place like a money-is-the-bottom-line business, the Cottage Rose will lose some of its charm—if not all of it," she countered with a sharp raise of her chin.

He wanted to kiss it, then her lips, which at the moment had thinned into a straight line. He wanted to feel them, soft as marshmallows, melt beneath his. His mind fled the precarious state of her finances and centered, instead, on the woman beside him. She wore the same pistachio-striped top she'd had on the day he'd arrived here, the same skimpy white shorts. Her feet were bare, he noted, as she shifted in the chair and tucked one leg up under her delightful bottom. Her toenails were a pert shade of peppermint pink, and he longed to plant a kiss on each toe, then up the length of her silky leg.

"Is something wrong?" she asked, catching him in his reverie. She glanced down, then tugged on the hem of her shorts and edged them lower in a self-consious gesture, an attempt at modesty that failed gloriously.

"Just, uh, admiring your pink polish." Among other things, he added silently—and more truthfully.

He forced his attention back to the records in front of him. It took him a major moment to regain his train of thought, but finally he did. "There's no way to compute your projected earnings for the coming months, let alone the next year," he said. "But your expenses are considerable, even without any future calamity befalling this old place—"

"Wash your mouth out with soap, Josh Alexander. Nothing else will go wrong with this house—at least not this season." She rapped her knuckles on wood for good measure.

He grinned. "Okay, but even without a major repair, even with a good-to-excellent occupancy rate, it's going to be tight."

She arched one eyebrow. "I hardly needed someone with your fancy credentials to tell me that."

"Hey, people pay good money for my advice," he defended. "The least you could be is grateful. Now, if you'll close that smart mouth of yours, I'll offer a few suggestions."

"Offer away."

"Thank you." He took a piece of paper and jotted down his recommendations. "Number one—invest in some well-placed ads," he outlined in his best adviser voice. This brought a soft, disgruntled snort, which he decided to ignore. "Number two—minimize your expenses by cutting out the frills—"

"No frill cutting. Not for the Cottage Rose. The extras are what give the place its charm, its—"

He tossed down his pen. "Are you going to take my advice or not?"

"I agreed to listen. Not take."

He never got to recommendation three. Her mouth puckered delightfully in front of him. He leaned over to taste the pout on it. He couldn't help himself. Lindsay drove him wild with wanting her. These past few days of keeping hands off, of playing it her way, had taken its toll on him. Hell, he wasn't a saint. Men weren't cut out for the role. Or didn't she realize that?

His hands cupped the sides of her face, drawing her deeper into the kiss. His tongue traced the silken outline of her bottom lip, then the top, until he heard her soft gasp of pleasure. His own pleasure climbed the Richter scale.

Her cheeks felt feverish beneath his palms. A tiny pulse at the side of her neck beat as rapidly as a hummingbird's wings beneath his thumb. Her arms curved around him, her hands on his back, her soft breasts pressed against his chest, a tender vise from which only a crazy man would want to escape.

Lindsay hadn't wanted this to happen, knew that if it did, her resolve to distance herself from this man would evaporate like the early-morning mist.

He felt so good beneath her hands as she ran them over the hard muscles in his back. What his mouth was doing to hers destroyed her sanity, her ability to reason. Her lips parted, and his tongue parried with hers in a frantic dance of need. An undeniable heat curled low in her body and quickly spread to her limbs, rendering them languid.

Why did this feel so right, so perfect, when a half moment before, her head had told her this couldn't be? She knew without a doubt that no man would stir her soul as Josh did, that even after he'd left Folly, her heart would forever be his.

Josh kissed the pulse in her neck that now beat more feverishly. For him? The thought sent his own pulses racing. He followed the curve of her throat, his lips seeking her sweetness.

"Lindsay..." He whispered her name against her softness. He wanted her for his own. His own temptress. His enchantress.

He drew back and ran a finger over her slightly swollen lips. She trembled under his touch. "Lindsay, how many reservations do you have for next week?" he asked quietly.

She gave a small laugh. "Are we back to my finances again?"

"No, I'm just checking on the availability of my room. I want to extend my vacation."

Her mouth formed the prettiest gape he'd ever seen, and he bent to kiss her again.

Chapter Eight

Snip. Snip. Snip. Lindsay clipped at the backyard hedge with her shears, frightening a bird into flight. When had she fallen headlong in love with the man? How had it happened?

Snip. Snip. Snip. The more time they spent with each other, the harder it would be to say goodbye. These past few days were proof of that.

Snip. Snip. Since Josh had announced that he was staying on Folly another week, they'd spent more and more time together. They'd scuba dived off Wilder's Point. They'd found secluded places to picnic. They'd shared kisses, her body aching for more, aching for him to make love to her. But that was a temptation she couldn't give in to. How would she be able to say goodbye to him when the time came? How would she be able to live with the memories of that intimacy? No, making love with Josh was a complication she couldn't allow in her life.

Snip. Snip. Snip. Snip. She'd had a few more days of seeing him get up in the morning, sit across from her at breakfast. They'd had time for a few more little talks alone together in the quiet of the evening. But she trembled with the knowledge that they were only living on borrowed time. Josh would leave, as she knew he must, and her life would be desolately empty without him.

He was in her kitchen making phone calls. He'd been there half the afternoon. It seemed he couldn't stay away from business for longer than a day, two at the most. Her workaholic was far from cured.

Had she hoped that Folly would change him? That his company, his life on the mainland, wouldn't be quite so important? That he'd have room in his life for her? Still, he'd made progress, she tried to convince herself. Rome wasn't built in a day, after all.

Snip—

"What are you doing to that hedge, girl?"

Lindsay whirled around to see Henry Potter standing behind her, his white legs sticking out from a pair of wild plaid shorts.

"The haircut you're giving that shrub reminds me of a few Stella's given me. Back when I had hair, that is." He chortled. "I'd look in the mirror and be sure she was mad at me for something."

Wiping the sweat from her forehead with the back of her hand, Lindsay glanced at the hedge's jagged outline. "It does look like I've been taking my frustrations out on it," she admitted.

"This wouldn't have anything to do with Joshua, would it?" Henry probed.

"Josh? No. Why would it?"

Henry only chuckled.

Lindsay blushed. She'd never noticed living in the Cottage Rose was like living in a fish bowl—at least until now. Everything she did, every action, was open to view by her guests. Were her feelings also as obvious to them?

She glanced down at the book Henry clutched in his hand. "What's this, a new bird guide?" she asked, an attempt to change the subject.

"Those nice girls gave it to me. Tanya and Steffie. Such sweet things."

Lindsay smiled, surprised at her young guests' thoughtful gesture.

"They bought something for Joshua, too."

"Oh." This piqued her interest undeniably. The girls had continued to bat their eyelashes at Josh—*and* pout over the amount of time he'd been spending with Lindsay. "What did they give him?"

"He's wearing it. You'll see," Henry answered mysteriously. "Ah, here he comes now. Well, I'll, uh, leave you two alone. Stella and I have a date—at the ice-cream parlor."

Lindsay had to smile. There was a closeness between Henry and Stella that was enviable. They were always there for each other, growing old together, yet acting as young as kids, too.

"Don't let her get near you with those shears, my boy," he warned Josh, then gave him a friendly jab in the rib-cage and headed into the house in search of his wife.

Tanya and Steffie were definitely into the gift-giving mood, she decided as she watched Josh stride closer. Molded to his broad, muscled chest was a T-shirt that read: On a Scale Of One To Ten, This Body Is *Perfect!* Lindsay had caught them eyeing that perfect body on more than one occasion...but then, she could hardly blame them. The man was gorgeous.

Josh gave her a nuzzling kind of kiss on her neck, which sent shivers down her spine. "What did Henry mean about the shears?" he asked. Then he spied the hedge she'd been butchering and laughed long and deep.

If it wasn't such a sexy, male sound, she'd have hated him for it. "I just need to even it out a little," she defended, giving the bush another snip or two.

"Yeah...right."

He took the shears and dropped them to the grass, then gave her a long, branding kiss, this one on her lips. When he released her, she felt giddy and had to hold on to him until the world steadied itself.

"I have something I need to talk to you about tonight," he murmured. "I made dinner reservations for us at the Surfside."

She drew back and stared at him in surprise. The Surfside was Folly's most intimate restaurant, with candlelit tables overlooking the rough, windward surf, a place for lovers' trysts, a place for marriage proposals.

She trembled slightly, not entirely sure why—except that there was something in his tone.... "What...what do you need to talk to me about?"

"Tonight." He smiled and ran a finger over her lower lip, the light touch inflaming her senses. "We'll talk about it tonight."

Lindsay sank down into the silky bubbles in the big claw-footed tub, pondering the evening ahead of her. What did Josh want to talk to her about? And why over candlelight? Was he going to suggest they become lovers?

Or was tonight perhaps goodbye? Did he intend to tell her he was leaving, that he couldn't stay longer on Folly after all, that pressing business called him back early?

A shiver ran through her and she slid down further into the tub. Maybe she'd just stay here until her skin shriveled. She didn't want to hear Josh say the words that would condemn her to existence without him.

She hadn't wanted to fall in love with him, but she had. And she wasn't sure how she would live with the consequences of that.

When the water cooled, she stepped out of the tub onto a fuzzy peach bath mat and toweled herself dry. Perhaps she was jumping to wrong conclusions here. What he wanted to talk to her about might not be anything as traumatic as goodbye. Yes, she decided, she wouldn't let fear ruin their evening.

For tonight she would bury deep the fact that they were so different from each other, that they'd each set different goals in their lives, that an unforgiving sea separated their worlds. Tonight she would just enjoy the dinner, the view of the surf, the moonlight and the candlelight—and Josh.

She wanted to walk along the beach, hand in hand with him, breathing in his scent, feeling the roughness of his cheek against hers, knowing that he was real, that he existed, that they'd had this brief time together.

And if he wants to make love to you? the other possibility reared its head. Heat raced through her veins and something else...unfulfilled need. The need to have him love her, long and thoroughly. Despite the memories she would live with once he'd gone?

Yes, despite the memories.

She slipped into her light robe and belted it tightly around her. Her reflection gazed back at her from the mirror, her face flushed with color. She brushed a strand of hair away from her cheek. She wasn't at all sure she'd have the strength to say no to him tonight in the moonlight.

Josh paced the front parlor, waiting for Lindsay. He'd told her eight o'clock, and it was already—he glanced at the clock—already one minute past.

He wanted tonight to be special for them, but particularly for Lindsay. He didn't know when or how she'd become so important to him, but she had. Even waiting for her to show for their date had him impatient for the sight of her.

He had it bad.

Very bad.

But he couldn't help it. Lindsay made the blood pound in his veins.

He studied the clock again, then his own watch. Two minutes. Now she was two minutes late. He paced the length of the worn Persian carpet.

How would Lindsay take the surprise he had for her? He fingered the Victorian fringe on a lampshade. He was taking one hell of a chance. She could hate the idea. He'd spent all afternoon on the phone setting things up, but he could be going too far, too fast. Lindsay was the reluctant type, after all.

Maybe he would ply her with wine first, soften her up, set just the right mood. Then he'd tell her.

He was being selfish, he knew, but he wanted her on the mainland. With him. And this was one way....

What was keeping her? He checked his watch again. He was about to head down the hall and knock on her door, but at that moment the door opened. He stood staring at the vision before him.

"Wow!" he said, the single word woefully inadequate, but he was too awed to think of another. She was wearing a slim, mint-green sundress held up by two tiny straps, straps that he'd have great difficulty leaving alone tonight. He let his gaze linger at each place the dress hugged her slender frame, her soft, rounded breasts with just the tiniest amount of tempting cleavage showing, her narrowed waist that invited a man's hand, her slightly flared hips.

She'd loosened her hair from its afternoon braid and it tumbled to her shoulders like a silvery waterfall. Later. Later, he'd tangle his hands in it, bury his face in it, breathe in its scent.

"You changed from the T-shirt Tanya and Steffie gave you," she teased, running her slow gaze down the front of his open-necked shirt.

He glanced down at his attire. The relaxed island dress code didn't require a tie, but even without it he felt hot under the collar. Right now he wished he'd opted for the girls' crazy gift instead of this summer blazer he intended to shed at the first opportunity. "I can change back," he offered all too willingly.

She fingered a shirt button. "I think I like this better."

"You're not the tiniest bit jealous that those girls gave me a present and not you, are you?"

"Not in the least," she said with a curve of a smile.

He led her out the door. It was a beautiful evening, perfect for a short walk to catch one of the trolleys that ran to the far side of the island and the restaurant. During the day the trolleys made beach runs and also met each ferry that arrived and left Folly.

They found seats at the back, and Josh enjoyed watching Lindsay's hair flutter on the breeze as they rode. She was squeezed up against him, their hips touching. Her skirt had slid up above her knees a delicious few inches, and he tried to confine his gaze to the passing scenery instead of the scattering of freckles on her knees.

"Did you get all your business calls made today?" she asked.

It took him a moment to gather his thoughts. "Business calls, uh, yes. All taken care of," he said. They were business in a manner of speaking, he supposed. Part of his surprise for Lindsay. Again, he worried about how she'd react when he told her the news.

Lindsay leaned back against the seat and let the sea breeze that blew through the trolley wash over her. "I love the smell of the ocean," she said, breathing in deeply. "At night it has a different scent than it does during the day. I like the night smell best."

"You do?"

She nodded. "I love to walk along the shore in the evenings after the sun goes down."

His eyes were intent on her face. "After dinner we'll do just that, pretty Lindsay."

Her heart thudded against her rib cage. She wasn't at all sure that was a good idea. Her feelings tonight were attached to a very short fuse, and being alone with Josh in the moonlight could be just the spark to ignite them. "I don't know if we'll have the time. We might miss the last trolley back."

"Then we'll just take one of those unromantic cabs."

She laughed. The island's cab service, with its aging fleet of rattling taxis, did leave a lot to be desired. "You think of everything."

"I try to."

They'd reached the restaurant. The low, rambling building sat serenely on the cliff, shimmering like a jewel against the navy blue sea beyond. Golden candlelight poured through the windows, and the soft whisper of music wafted on the night breeze. The interior was cool and elegant, and every table had a view of the surf, floodlit at night.

The maître d' showed them to a quiet corner of the room. Since Folly was so small she knew everyone on the island but the restaurant hired so many mainlanders for the busy summer months that she didn't recognize either the maitre d' or their waiter.

A few Folly residents were patrons tonight, and she nodded to them as she and Josh settled into their seats. Perhaps this wasn't a good idea, she thought as she picked up the menu, feeling their gazes roam over her and the man she was with. Folly residents were a curious bunch. There wasn't a whole lot to gossip about most of the time, but she had the feeling that after tonight she and Josh would become the topic of their speculation.

Josh looked intriguingly male in his white summer blazer and navy slacks. The wind had ruffled his hair. He'd dragged a hand through it, which had done little to tame the thick, wavy curls.

"What's good here?" he asked, glancing up from his menu to catch her gaze on him.

"Uhh..." She corralled her woolgathering thoughts. "Lobster is the specialty, but everything's wonderful."

Lindsay was as skittish as she was beautiful tonight, Josh thought. Skittish was not the way he wanted her. "And the wine?" he asked, remembering his resolve to soften her up, set the right mood for their evening before he sprang his surprise.

"I've only tried their Chardonnay. It's very good."

"Then Chardonnay it is." He ordered the wine, lobster tails for them both, then settled back in his chair, his eyes on Lindsay.

"What did you want to talk to me about?" she asked.

He enjoyed the way she worried her lower lip with her even white teeth. For a moment he imagined those teeth nipping at his skin, driving him insane with passion. He sighed with relief when the waiter brought their wine, thus banishing the naughty image. He busied himself with sampling the vintage, then nodded his approval to the waiter. He was saved from answering Lindsay's question until the waiter left. But when he did, the question was still there in her big blue-green eyes.

"Later," he said. "Those people over there are staring at us."

Lindsay gave a small laugh. She knew without turning around which people he meant. "Folly's a small island, and when some strange man takes me to dinner, the natives are naturally curious."

"I didn't realize I was a strange man." He frowned in feigned umbrage.

"You know what I mean. You're a...curiosity. Sorry, that's not what I meant, either."

"I hope not. I hope I'm more than a curiosity to you."

Lindsay swallowed hard. He was becoming everything to her. She no longer felt in control. Josh had her spinning in circles. He had her hoping they could put off the inevitable, that his time on Folly would never come to an end. She took a sip of her wine and studied him over the glass.

His dark eyes watched her with lively interest, making her feel like she was the center of his attention. It was a look she wished she could capture and save, to pluck from her memory some lonely night when he was gone. "What are your dreams, Lindsay?" he asked. "Tell me about them."

She lowered her lashes, his question catching her by surprise. "Dreams? As in..."

"As in wishes," he clarified.

"For the Cottage Rose?"

"No, Lindsay. For you."

"Oh." She thought for a moment, not sure what to answer, how much to tell him. She took another sip of wine and let the liquid melt through her. When she set it down, he took her hand, enveloping it in the heat of his. "I've never tried to put it into words." She paused, feeling like see-through crystal, everything about herself visible to him. "Fulfillment, I suppose. Children—someday. A husband who'll be there for me, who I can be there for." He made small circles on her palm, making it difficult for her to think.

"How many children?" he asked, his voice all whispery, feathering across her senses.

"A half dozen would be nice." She grinned. "But two would be a handful, I'm sure. I just don't want *one* child. I don't want a child to grow up alone."

Josh saw a moment of pain in her eyes. Lindsay's childhood had been lonely at times. In spite of her Aunt Rose. "And what about your paintings? Are they a part of that fulfillment?"

"My art is relaxation, my inner peace, what makes everything seem right in the world—"

Just then the waiter interrupted with their food, effectively cutting off their conversation.

"What about you?" she asked when they were once again alone. "Tell me your dreams."

Josh would have preferred talking about Lindsay. She was so warm, so open, except for the small part of her she was hesitant to let him see. "I'm not sure I have dreams, they're more like goals." He studied the lobster on his plate with anticipation. It was one of the largest he'd ever been served. "I have this blueprint for success. A timetable for when I want to accomplish what in my life." He picked up his fork and started in on the lobster.

When he glanced up, he found Lindsay's forehead pleated in a troubled frown. "I know, I know—my partners give me that same look. But that's the way I am, Lindsay. Focused, singleminded—"

"Driven."

She made the word sound like a vice instead of a virtue. "Yes, even driven. Look, Lindsay, I've proved I could come here to Folly, that I could relax—"

"Is that what this dinner is? Proof you can relax?" Her eyes glazed over, stricken with pain. She drew her hand away from his, knotting it tensely. Her voice was low, injured. "Is that what I am, too? Proof you can take your mind off business long enough to—"

"No! Dammit, Lindsay, no!" This wasn't the way he wanted this evening to go. "I planned this dinner as a celebration."

"A celebration?" She studied him for a long considering moment. "You...you were on the phone all afternoon. Is that what you're celebrating?"

"Not me, Lindsay. Us. It's what we're celebrating."

"Then maybe you'd better let me in on it."

"I wanted it to be a surprise, a special surprise for you. But it can wait until after dinner." He didn't want to tell her now, not this way, not when she was all prickly. "We'll grab a bottle of champagne, take that walk along the beach. I'll tell you then." He went back to his lobster, hoping she would do the same.

His hopes were unfounded. She leaned forward, her blue-green eyes cemented on him. "Josh, if this surprise involves me, then I think you'd better tell me what it is. Now."

How had his well-intentioned evening gone so awry? He laid down his fork, eyeing his lobster with one final lingering glance and picked up his wineglass, downing a hefty swallow. He reached for her hand, but she withdrew it to her lap. "It has to do with dreams," he said, hoping to ease into his explanation.

"Dreams?"

There was no other way to tell her except all-out. "Lindsay, I've arranged an exhibit for you. A showing of your paintings at a small gallery in Boston. That's what I was doing on the phone today, arranging everything."

Lindsay stared at him in stunned disbelief. Certainly she hadn't heard what she thought she'd heard from his lips. She swallowed the rising knot in her throat. Her breath burned in her chest. She wanted to scream, she wanted to run, she wanted to beat her fists against him. Her voice came out in a shaky gasp. "You did that—without asking me?"

How could he? How could he do such a thing? Her paintings were personal, a part of herself, and she would choose whether or not to show them to the world.

"Lindsay, I understand your reluctance—"

"Oh, do you? Do you understand anything at all about me?"

"I understand that you have talent, lots of it, that you could be a success in the art world—"

She didn't want success. Success got in the way of too many other things—important things. She knew. She'd watched her mother put the success of her business ahead of all else, vacations, holidays—a little girl's needs.

She pushed aside the memory. That was the past. She had the present to deal with. And the future, a future with other priorities. "You can cancel whatever plans you've made, I'm not interested."

"Lindsay, I know I took you by surprise with this, but just think about it. An exhibit at a small but renowned Boston gallery, that's nothing to sneeze at."

If he was waiting for her gratitude, he'd have a long wait. His "surprise" only pointed out what she'd known from the beginning. They were different, too different for there ever to be anything lasting between them. And she was a fool to think there could have been.

Josh was ambitious. By his own admission, driven. He wanted the world on a string. And she suspected he would get it. But she wasn't like that. It wasn't what she wanted. And maybe what she wanted was harder to get—a forever kind of love, a being-there-for-the-other kind of love.

She thought of Henry and Stella, holding hands through life, through the ups and downs, the happiness, the heartaches. That's what she wanted—and what she knew Josh couldn't give her.

She died a little inside at the painful realization.

Daydreams. Wishful thinking, that's all she'd really had. But tonight was reality, painful reality.

She glanced down at the plate she'd barely touched. She saw the reflection of the candle on their table, twinkling against her wineglass. She heard the murmurs, the laughter, of the other patrons around her, the soft strains of the music in the background. She didn't belong here.

She pushed back her chair and got unsteadily to her feet. "I have to get out of here. I—I'm sorry." She didn't know what she was sorry for. For what could have been? That they viewed the world from opposite poles?

Her throat burned with the tears she held back. She wouldn't let them spill, not here in this restaurant in front of Folly's residents, not here in front of Josh.

"Lindsay..." Josh was on his feet.

She opened her mouth to say something—what, she didn't know—but no words came out. Instead, she snatched up her purse, then turned and fled.

"Lindsay..."

"Is everything all right, sir?" The waiter was at his side, wearing the solicitous face of a funeral director.

"What? Oh, uh, yes, the lady just remembered an appointment," he lied. He extracted enough bills from his wallet to cover the check and a sizable tip. "I'd better see her home."

He wanted to take back what he'd done. Lindsay was so private about her work, so guarded. He should have known she'd hate the idea—and resent even more his arranging anything without her knowledge.

He received stares as he hurried through the restaurant. He nearly bolted into a table of water goblets in his haste. But he had to reach Lindsay, tell her how wrong he'd been. He had to tell her that he was sorry. About everything. If he lived to be a hundred and two, he'd never forget the pain he saw shimmering in her eyes.

He knew he'd angered her, but he'd hurt her as well—for some reason he didn't quite understand. He didn't know Lindsay, not really, not deep-in-his-heart know her.

And now he wasn't sure Lindsay would let him know her or even let him within ten feet of her.

He reached the door and broke out into the night. Lindsay was nowhere in sight. The beach. Maybe she'd gone to the beach.

"If you're looking for the lady, she caught the trolley."

Josh whirled around to find the maître d' wearing the same anxious face he'd seen on the waiter a few moments before.

"Is everything all right?"

Josh wasn't going through his story again. "When's the next trolley?" he asked the man brusquely.

"Twenty minutes."

Too long. "How about a cab?"

"Oh, they'd all be at the ferry landing. It docks about now."

Josh raked a hand through his hair. Damn this island, this remote, inconvenient island.

Chapter Nine

Lindsay hugged the rail at the back of the trolley and let the tears flow. She'd get over it, she told herself between gulps of air. She'd get over Josh. Easily. Because he'd only been a fantasy, a daydream. The man she'd thought she loved didn't exist, except as a figment of her imagination. A summer guest who'd very nearly stolen her heart. But it was there, intact. Bruised a little, yes, but intact.

Then why did it hurt so much? Why did she feel as though nothing would ever be right again?

She faced the night, out the back of the trolley, not wanting the few passengers to see her tears. Couples. Late at night the trolley only carried couples, happy, laughing, in love. She was the only single rider.

She wrapped her arms around herself and wondered when the night chill had settled in. The wind chapped her face, damp with tears, whipped the ends of her hair, slapping them across her cheeks. She barely felt any of it. She only felt the pain that shredded her heart into ribbons.

Josh had his life all mapped out—his blueprint for success. But where in his scheme of things was there room for love? Marriage? Children? Those were successes, too—the only kind that mattered.

He'd wanted to give her a gallery showing, but her art was an expression of her soul. She couldn't bare it to the world. And that was something she didn't think he could understand. Not a man who'd grown up competing for everything.

Even coming here to Folly had been a contest of sorts for him. He'd had something to prove, that he could spend two weeks here, on this isolated island, at the end of the world. And he'd done that, he'd proved his mettle. He could go home now, with one more success notched into his belt.

It seemed forever before the trolley reached its stop. She got off and walked the short block to the Cottage Rose. The place was ablaze with lights. Every guest was at home. She couldn't let them see her tears. She had to hold her head up, especially in front of the perceptive Henry. She dried her eyes with the back of her hand, squared her shoulders, pinning them back by sheer force of will.

She'd known pain before—but Aunt Rose had always been there for her, to soften it and ease the hurt. Lindsay wished she were there now, with her open arms, her wise words.

Tacking on a smile, she braved the front door.

Henry greeted her inside. "There you are. We were about to play a game of cards. Everyone's in the kitchen. Even Tanya and Steffie."

Lindsay couldn't do this. She didn't have the courage. Not tonight. Not when the pain of her reality was so fresh. She needed some time alone, time for the numbness to take hold. Tomorrow. Tomorrow she'd be fine.

Henry was studying her curiously, and he would be like a dog worrying a bone if he suspected she was hurting. She didn't want him to know. Or the others. "Thanks, anyway, Henry, but I'm a little tired. I think I'll turn in early."

She remembered her hostess duties. "Feel free to make coffee, and if you want a late snack, there's a three-layer fudge cake I baked this afternoon."

Josh had told her she was a nurturer—to her soul. And she realized he was right, but tonight that talent came hard. Tonight she was the one who needed the nurturing.

"Is everything all right, pretty one, you look a little pale?"

She put as much brightness in her smile as she could manage. "I'm okay. Go and play your game of cards."

She started for her bedroom, but didn't get far.

"I thought you and Joshua had plans tonight," Henry called to her down the hallway.

Her hand froze on the doorknob to her bedroom, where the privacy inside offered escape. "Our plans changed," she said. So had her hopes, so had her life. "Good night, Henry."

She pushed open the door and shut it behind her, then let the tears fall.

Josh kicked his cursed backside every step of the long walk back home. Home? Why did he think of it as that? Because Lindsay was there? Because it was warm and inviting? In spite of Henry, in spite of Tanya and Steffie? Yes, even filled with her collection of house-guests, it was a haven, a refuge.

He wished he were there right now.

His right shoe pinched and he relished the pain, feeling he deserved it. It had been more than two weeks since he'd had on the uncomfortable shoes, more than two weeks since he'd come to Folly, banished from the real world. And now he wasn't sure which was the real world. Lindsay had him so confused. She had him sorting through his priorities like they were a deck of cards.

And every time he shuffled through them, he came out the Joker.

He gave a low, cynical laugh and kicked at a stone.

How many miles had he come? The road was little more than a path, but it was shorter than the route that followed the shoreline.

The night was cool; still he'd worked up a sweat. Sand clung to his pant legs and there was at least a bucketful in each shoe. He'd shed his blazer after the first half mile, tossing it over one shoulder, a forgotten reminder of their special evening gone sour. He'd hoped for a romantic walk along the beach with Lindsay, not this trek through the dunes alone.

But he'd blown it, blown everything. Would she even talk to him when he got there?

Lindsay was different. She was fragile. And she was private—with her life, with her work. He'd violated that privacy, stepped over the bounds. Big time. He'd forgotten she wasn't like any woman he'd ever known. And that very difference was why he'd fallen in love with her.

Whoaaa! That bombshell of a realization made him trip over a piece of driftwood in his path. He cursed. Colorfully. Was that what was causing such confusion in his well-plotted life?

He'd never been in love before. He was sure of it. He'd come dangerously close a time or two, but he'd always regained his perspective in time. But this had crept up on him. Broadsided him. Lindsay had broadsided him. She delighted and tantalized him. She frustrated and bewildered him.

And he didn't know what the hell he was going to do about it. At the moment she considered him lower than a creature that swam beneath pond scum and slept under rocks.

By the time he reached the Cottage Rose his feet wore blisters and his white blazer resembled the "before" picture in a laundry ad. He pushed open the front door.

Laughter greeted him, the sound coming from the kitchen. Feminine laughs. Henry's more generous guffaws. But not Lindsay's soft, warm delight.

Henry saw him when he rounded the corner into the kitchen. "Come in, join us," he invited. Then his eyes took in Josh's appearance. "What happened to you? Roll down a sand dune?"

This brought a round of laughter from the group.

"Something like that. Have you seen Lindsay?" Josh asked.

"She's gone off to bed," Henry told him.

"Thanks."

He stepped out of the kitchen and drew in a deep breath. He had to talk to her, whether or not she wanted to talk to him.

He started down the hallway to her room. No light shone under her door. He hesitated a moment, then rapped sharply. "Lindsay, may I come in? We need to talk."

"I'm asleep."

"You don't sound asleep."

"Well, I am."

"Lindsay..." He waited. This time there was silence. "Lindsay...I'm coming in." He tried the knob, then heard the old, heavy key in the lock fall to the floor on the opposite side.

He felt like a thief in the night. And it wasn't a feeling he liked. He'd never forced his attentions on any woman in his life, but Lindsay perceived him as some kind of a threat. She felt vulnerable. To him. Why else had she locked her door against him?

His jaw clenched and his hand opened and closed on the knob. He'd never encountered a locked door in the Cottage Rose, not even the front entry at night. In fact, he hadn't known the old locks had keys—until now.

He leaned a shoulder against the doorjamb. He felt damned silly having a conversation with a one-inch thick door, but he intended to have it. He had fences to mend, and Lindsay was going to listen.

"You want to call me a jerk? I'm guilty," he began, addressing a striation in the old wood. Lindsay had him doing any number of things he wouldn't have been caught dead doing before he met her.

"You're a jerk. Now go away so I can sleep," Lindsay replied from her spot on the other side. She'd been in bed, not asleep. She was certain sleep would elude her tonight. For many nights. But, as if against her will, she'd moved silently toward the door, toward the warmth of Josh on the other side.

Josh's heart lurched at the sound of her voice. It wasn't exactly a sweet whisper in his ear, but she'd at least spoken to him. After what he'd done, he had to be satisfied with that.

He planted both hands flat against the door, as if to reach out to the woman on the other side. "We're going to talk, Lindsay. I'd prefer to do that face-to-face."

He'd prefer to crash down the door, this barrier between them, take her into his arms and kiss away all the hurt he'd seen in her eyes earlier. Hold her all night, make love to her until she was gasping and begging for release. But he couldn't force his way into her life—not again. He'd done that when he'd tried to force her into an art showing she didn't want.

When he made love to Lindsay, he wanted her ready and willing. He swallowed hard. He was dying here on this side of the door. "Lindsay, are you there, do you hear me?"

"I hear you. So does everyone in the Cottage Rose, no doubt."

"Then let me in."

She couldn't do that. Seeing him would hurt too much. She'd be stronger tomorrow. Tomorrow she could treat him like any other guest. Why, when she'd found a man she was hopelessly in love with, did he have to be all wrong for her?

"I'm sorry, Lindsay. Sorry about tonight. I shouldn't have done what I did, I shouldn't have set up that exhibit without asking you first. It was just that you have such beautiful talent, and I was afraid you didn't know that. I...I thought that by getting you to the mainland, we could have more time together. I'm going to be there a lot, setting up the new office. Dammit, Lindsay, I wanted you there with me."

He held his breath. No sound came from the other side. She was there. He could smell her fragrance, soft and sweet and oh, so feminine. "Lindsay...do you hear me?"

Lindsay had heard him. Clearly. Tears prickled at her eyelids. She wouldn't cry again. She'd done enough of that in her life. She wouldn't cry over this man. But even as she vowed it, her throat clogged. Pain, fresh and new, gripped her again. She slumped against the door, hugging her arms to herself, and slowly sank to the floor.

"Lindsay..."

"Josh, go away."

"You're crying. Let me in."

"I'm not crying."

She wouldn't cry, not for a man who only wanted to fit her into some kind of time frame for his goals. He wanted her there while he set up his new office. Well, what about her life? What about the Cottage Rose? Did he really think she could drop everything that was important to her and rush off to Boston?

"Lindsay—let me see you. Let me in. Let me hold you, *show* you how sorry I am about tonight."

His words were soft, a lure, a temptation. She knew how his arms felt, she knew how he would show her he was sorry. He would make love to her...in this bed, tonight, moonlight bathing their nakedness, their passion.

Hadn't she dreamed it, hadn't she wanted it to happen—at least once before he left Folly? Once for her to hang on to, once for a memory so exquisitely beautiful.... But she knew that wouldn't solve anything.

She moved a few steps away from the door, as if she didn't trust herself not to pick up the key and open it, open it to Josh—and to more pain.

"This isn't about tonight, Josh. Not completely. It goes deeper than that. It's about who we are... and what we want for our lives."

Josh wanted Lindsay in his life, on the mainland, with him. He wanted to tell her he'd fallen in love with her, but he didn't want to tell her like this.

She'd moved away from the door. He could feel himself losing her. "Lindsay..." There was an edge of desperation in his voice, and he hated himself for it. "Lindsay, we have something between us, something special. Give it a chance, give *us* a chance."

"There is no *us*, there never was. We shouldn't have started this relationship. It won't work, it never could have worked. Don't you see that, Josh?"

Her voice was soft, muffled, as if coming from a distance. She'd moved farther away. She'd moved away from him, somewhere he couldn't reach her.

Maybe he would never be able to reach her.

That slow realization moved through him like ice through his veins. Lindsay couldn't leave Folly. She couldn't leave the Cottage Rose. Not for a showing in Boston. And not for him.

Her life and her heart were here. On this island. She was afraid to leave it, afraid to trust him, afraid to trust even in her talent. And he didn't know why.

He pictured her standing at the window, looking out at the night. Or maybe she sat huddled in the center of the bed, wrapped in herself. She couldn't live in his world, and he couldn't live in hers. That was the real truth of what she was saying.

He pushed himself away from the door, tamping down an overpowering need to pound his fists against it. He would, if he'd thought it would do any good. But it wouldn't.

He swallowed the bitter knot of regret lodged in his throat and found his voice. "Is this the way you want it then, Lindsay? Is this the end?"

She didn't answer him. Did he really think she would?

"Maybe you're right, maybe this never could have worked between us."

He waited for what seemed like an eternity, waited for her to refute his words, to take them back, to say he was wrong, that she was wrong, but again no sound came from the other side.

He dragged his hands through his hair, feeling all of tonight's frustration telescoped into that moment. There was nothing else to say, except good-night. "Go to sleep, pretty Lindsay. I—I won't bother you again."

Lindsay stood in the center of the room, her eyes on the door. She wanted to run to it and fling it open. She wanted to call him back, but she couldn't do that.

A tear streaked down her cheek, followed by another and then another. Soon her face was wet with them. She didn't bother to wipe them away. Only more would come.

A knot rose in Lindsay's throat when she saw the bulging tan suitcase by the front door the next morning—Josh's suitcase.

He was leaving.

Of course. He had to get back to the mainland, she knew. And he'd stayed more than long enough to win his bet.

She drew a shaky breath and turned toward the kitchen. He would need something to eat before he left. She wouldn't send a guest, any guest, on his way without sustenance.

By the time Josh found her a few minutes later, she was squeezing oranges for fresh juice. He startled her, and she spun around. Her heart slammed into her throat, colliding with the knot already lodged there.

He looked tired. Dark smudges of sleeplessness shadowed his eyes as if he'd been up most of the night. Because of her? Or had he stayed up late working?

He was dressed as he'd been the day he'd come, wearing a tie, a jacket. No doubt he planned to go into the office as soon as he reached the mainland. He would want to collect on his bet and get caught up on the work that had piled up while he was gone, of course.

"I'm checking out this morning," he said.

"I... I know. I saw your luggage. Of course, I'll refund the balance of your week's stay."

"No... You owe me nothing. I'd booked the room for the entire week."

She handed him a glass of juice. "The rolls are warming in the oven. I'll get you one." She turned away toward the oven.

"Lindsay... I don't want breakfast. I'm all packed, and the cab's been called." He set the glass down on the counter, untouched. "I... just came in here to... to say goodbye."

It was really over.

Lindsay's eyes lingered a moment on his face, as if to press the sight of it into her memory; then she looked away.

"Will you say goodbye to Henry and Stella and to the others for me?" he asked.

She nodded, unable to speak.

He stood there, looking at her as if he intended to say something more, but the noise of the taxi horn broke into the moment. This was it, this was goodbye. And it hurt more than she ever thought possible.

She willed herself not to cry, not to make a fool of herself, not to let him see her heart was shattering. She forced a smile. "Ha—have a safe trip."

She couldn't go with him to the door, couldn't see him walk down the front steps to the cab waiting to take him out of her life. She turned and glanced out the window, at the hammock swinging lightly in the wind, watching the rhythmic sway until she heard the front door shut. She squeezed her eyes closed to shutter the tears.

Her other guests would be coming down for breakfast any minute, and she didn't want them to catch her crying. Her life would go on as before. Somehow.

Josh's so-called friends, his two ignoble partners, gathered around his desk, declaring their disbelief at his successfully completed mission, he'd survived the two weeks on quiet Folly Island.

Tom slapped him on the back. "I didn't think you could do it," he admitted, "but you proved me wrong."

"Yeah," Cliff rejoined, "I gave you three days, tops, and you'd come crawling back here, begging for our mercy."

Josh frowned malevolently at the pair. He'd had the last laugh, but he didn't feel at all like laughing. He'd won the bet, but the thrill of winning tasted like ashes in his mouth. He could expand the company as he'd planned, but even that had lost its appeal.

"Hey, how about we pop the cork on a bottle of champagne and you tell us how you did it," Tom suggested.

Josh's frown darkened. "Why don't the two of you just get the hell out of my office, so I can get some work done."

He enjoyed the look of stunned surprise on their faces. He wasn't feeling at all hospitable—or charitable—at the moment. If they hadn't sent him to Folly, he wouldn't have met Lindsay, and if he hadn't met Lindsay, he wouldn't be sitting here now, missing her with an ache that could cut him in two.

"Come on, Tom," Cliff urged. "He's like a bear with a thorn in its paw. And I, for one, don't want to be on the end of his bite."

When they'd left, Josh returned to his work—or rather, he'd tried to. Most of the time he sat and brooded as he'd done off and on throughout the day. He'd come directly here after leaving Folly. His suitcase sat by his office door, a mocking reminder of his enforced holiday. He tapped his pen against his desk and thought about what he'd left behind.

Lindsay, with her sweet ways, her blue-green eyes that reminded him of the sea, her smile that made him feel like the morning sun shone on him, her arms circling his neck, her soft, rounded breasts pressed against him—he was torturing himself with the memory. He shoved back his chair and strode to the window.

Dusk was settling over Hyannis. White sails still dotted the darkening ocean. His gaze hovered on the horizon, to where Folly lay just beyond, just out of his sight.

Out of his reach.

He reminded himself this was the way Lindsay wanted it. She could never bring herself to leave her island, to come to him. He knew that. What he didn't know was why—why didn't she trust him enough to believe he could make her happy? What was it that she feared? He'd seen something there, in her eyes, more than once. Just when she might have been his she would pull back, draw away from him—and he didn't know why.

But maybe it was for the best. Dammit, he had a life here, a life that, up until now, he'd liked. He had the company, he was the success he'd wanted to be. He'd even proved to his vile partners—and to himself—that he could relax on occasion. Even if that occasion had ended up being his undoing.

Well, it was time to get back to business. He had a new office to open in Boston for starters. He had to put Lindsay—and what couldn't be—out of his mind.

Lindsay greeted her new guests and led them upstairs to their rooms. This morning she'd waved goodbye to Henry and Stella, who'd left on the early ferry back to the mainland. The girls, Tanya and Steffie, had left the day before.

She'd kept Josh's room empty, unable to bring herself to fill it with a new guest. She'd even crept upstairs one night and slept in his bed, wanting, *needing*, to feel his presence, but the vacant room seemed to mock her.

She'd gone through the closet, searching for a trace of him, something he might have left behind, something to prove he'd been there, but bare hangers reminded her he'd gone. She'd opened the dresser drawers one by one. In the last one she'd found a button, a simple shirt button, and it had sent her into another crying jag. When she'd stopped, she'd stuck it into the pocket of her robe and returned to her own room and her own bed.

Josh was gone. And he wouldn't be back. She'd sent him away because she was afraid, afraid he couldn't offer her the kind of future she needed. The forever kind of future she wanted for herself—for her children one day.

The Cottage Rose was nearly full—with new patrons. She only had Josh's room left to fill—and very soon it, too, would be occupied. Reality had intruded when the owner of one of the other guest houses had phoned, hoping Lindsay might have a vacancy for a couple looking for a quiet place. Lindsay knew she had to offer them the accommodation. She couldn't turn them aside, not for a silly reason like not wanting to use the room because it had been Josh's.

Josh wasn't coming back. She hadn't expected him to.

"If you need anything, I'm right downstairs," she told her new residents. "And if you're interested in a tour of the island—" she felt her throat catch slightly, but forced herself to go on "—I have brochures outlining what's available."

Life would go on, she told herself as she crept back down the old staircase. Her tears had all been spent. She had no more in her.

But that was something she knew she didn't quite believe.

Chapter Ten

Josh wasn't at all sure why he was on this cursed ferry—except to prove to himself that he could kick back and relax on the long, damnably slow ride to Folly.

And why was he headed to Folly in the first place? his inner mind wanted to know.

He wasn't at all sure about that, either. Lindsay didn't want to see him. He was certain of that. Had he begun to hope that maybe, just maybe, she might have changed her mind? That the past two weeks had been as miserable for her as they'd been for him?

He'd thought work would cure all. He'd plunged into plans to expand the company into Boston. He'd even looked into the possibility of New York as a third location. It had been the next step on his timetable for success, his next intended achievement. But the achievement he'd expected would bring such joy to his life had rung hollow, instead.

And all because of Lindsay. She had affected his perspective on everything lately. She had him going in crazy directions. Hell, she even had him sitting on this damned ferry, with his feet propped on the rail, soaking up the sun over the Atlantic along with the salt spray that slapped against his face. And why? Just to see if he could relax.

At the moment he felt far from relaxed. He also felt a little foolish at having decided to take off for the weekend on the spur of the moment. On a whim. He didn't have luggage. He didn't even have reservations anywhere.

He doubted Lindsay would put him up—even if she had a bed available. And she damned well wouldn't let him share hers. If she knew he was even on the island, she'd probably send him back on the first boat.

The sound of the ferry whistle interrupted his train of thought. They'd just rounded Wilder's Point. They'd be docking soon.

He found himself searching through the trees and the rooftops for sight of the Cottage Rose. Now that he was almost there, he didn't know what to do. Did he just present himself at her front door?

What would he say to her? Nothing had changed between them, except the knowledge that living without her for the rest of his life would be pure hell.

Maybe he would have a talk with Doc first. Wise old Doc. He'd tell him he needed a fast cure for a broken heart—if there was one. Maybe Doc would have the solution to a problem that didn't seem to have any solution.

He was off the ferry and through the disembarking crowd quickly. With no luggage to claim, he started off down the wharf toward town. The sun overhead was warm. He shed the blue Windbreaker he'd worn on the ferry and tied the sleeves of it around his waist.

The narrow streets were filled with tourists, but he left them behind when he reached the dusty beach road that led to Doc's cottage. It was the last one at the end of the road, old and rambling, with green painted shutters and a weathered stone chimney reaching skyward.

He found Doc pruning his prized roses. The old physician glanced up and peered through his glasses to see who was coming, then peeled them off and wiped the sweat from his forehead before planting them back on his nose again.

Josh waved and called out to him.

"That you, Josh. Well, Lordeeee. Lindsay said you'd gone back to the mainland. I hope you made that appointment with your own doctor back home, had that thorough physical we talked about."

"My secretary set it up for me. It's next week, I think, but I feel fine."

Doc studied him carefully as he neared. "You sure? You don't look all that hot to me. Peaked around the eyes. You working too hard again?" It was not a gentle scolding. There was a bite to his words.

Josh brushed it aside, but Doc wasn't swayed.

"Now look here, Josh Alexander, I don't like it one bit when people don't heed my advice. I heard you'd decided to stay another week, then up and left early. What was that all about?" Doc tucked his pruning shears in his back pocket and led Josh to a pair of tall-backed wooden lawn chairs in the shade of an old maple. It had a view of the beach and the ocean beyond.

Prime real estate. Lindsay had told him it had been in the Tobias family since the whaling days.

Josh put up his hands in a defensive gesture. "I'm not working too hard. It's just...just that I haven't exactly been sleeping well lately."

"Aha!"

"Aha? What does that mean?" Josh frowned over at Doc, who had his antennae on medical alert.

Old doctors didn't die, they just hung around to poke and prod anyone who held still long enough for them to do so.

Josh was beginning to wish he hadn't come.

"It means I was right. Something happened between you and Lindsay. She has that same...haunted look you do. Peaked around the eyes. Diagnosis— she's in love and doesn't know what to do about it."

The crusty old man was wrong there. Lindsay was not in love—unless she'd met someone in the past few weeks. That thought made his heart lurch. Could she have forgotten him? So soon? He sat up straighter in the uncomfortable lawn chair. "When...when did you see her last?"

"Day before yesterday." Doc took off his glasses and polished them slowly with a big handkerchief. "I think you two need to talk about a few things."

Josh shook his head. "I don't think she wants to see me."

Doc pondered that for a moment; then his eyes narrowed. "Maybe you'd better tell me why not."

Josh squirmed under the man's gaze. He wasn't eager to relate the details of his last evening with Lindsay. Doc was very protective of her and would no doubt have a few choice remarks about Josh's intelligence when he learned about the art showing that he had planned for her as a surprise—the surprise that had been the start of the night's downhill slide to its painful conclusion.

He should have thought better about coming here. But now that he had, there was no getting out of it. If he wanted Doc's sage advice, he would have to tell him the whole story. He drew in a courageous breath and began.

To his credit, Doc listened noncommittally. His thick white brows rose occasionally. They also plunged to a pointed V over the bridge of his nose a dangerous time or two, but he reserved all comment until Josh had finished. Then he let out a wearied sigh and shook his head.

"I have to give you your due," he said. "In the history of every foolish thing man has ever tried to do for a woman, that is the—"

"Hey! You don't have to say it." Josh jolted from his seat, looking affronted.

Jamming his hands into the pockets of his cutoffs, he turned and faced Doc with a sharp frown. "Look," he said, "I came here to find out a few things about Lindsay, not have my prowess with women maligned."

"Point taken," Doc replied. "And I sure hope you two can work out your differences, find some common ground, though that won't be easy. The way I see it, that girl's been downright miserable since you left."

Josh sat down next to Doc again. That brought him a small ray of hope. But knowing how awful he'd felt the past two weeks, he wouldn't wish that on his worst enemy. He couldn't eat, couldn't sleep, couldn't think. He couldn't do anything that required physical or mental coordination.

"She's hurting?"

"She's hurting. I've known Lindsay since she was a little girl, and I don't like seeing her like this. She's already had enough pain in her life."

And Josh had inadvertently added to it, he knew.

Something he wasn't at all proud of.

Doc eyed him warily. "Do you love her?" he asked bluntly.

Josh nodded without hesitation. "I do, but love doesn't seem to solve the differences between us." He got up from his chair, raking a hand through his hair, feeling his desperation to a new depth. He felt restless, lost.

"How much has Lindsay told you about her life?"

Josh turned and looked at Doc. "Not much. That her father died when she was very young, that her Aunt Rose raised her. I know her father painted and that Lindsay got her rare talent from him. I know that Folly seems to be her refuge and I doubt... I doubt that she can ever bring herself to leave it."

"Few ever can, not once the island gets its hold on you," Doc said prophetically.

Josh gave a ragged sigh. That was not what he wanted to hear.

"I'm not sure you're the kind of man Lindsay needs in her life, but her heart seems to have tripped over you. But then, whoever said love was easy—or that it made a whip of sense?"

Josh frowned. "What do you mean, I'm not the kind of man she needs in her life?"

"I'm not sure you can give her what she needs most. Sit down, Josh, and listen. Listen good."

Josh took his seat. "I'm listening." He kept his sharp gaze on Doc.

"Lindsay spent her summers here when she was a little girl. Every summer. She was brightness and sunshine. She was happy. That was before her father was killed in that awful car accident and Lindsay's world changed."

Josh sat on the edge of the lawn chair, wanting to hear about this side of Lindsay he didn't know, yet dreading it, too.

Doc drawled on with his story. Josh listened, afraid the revelation would end his hopes, that it would prove the obstacles in their path were too insurmountable. "Lindsay's mother went to the mainland to work, leaving Lindsay here with Rose," he said. "Lindsay understood, even though she was very young, that there wasn't much employment here on Folly. There still isn't. This is a quiet place. And it was too quiet for a woman like Lindsay's mother."

The parallel Doc was drawing struck Josh in the gut with the impact of a hard fist to the midsection. He could see how Lindsay could equate his own ambition to that of her mother's, his own need to be on the mainland to her mother's need.

"Her mother put in long hours at the auction house where she worked," Doc went on. "Weekends, too. Eventually the company became hers. It wasn't exactly Sotheby's, but she began to build it into a prestigious establishment."

"And Lindsay was forgotten in the bargain," Josh said, feeling the extent of her pain, understanding now the sadness he'd seen in her eyes.

He let out a ragged sigh. He'd added to Lindsay's pain when he'd tried to force a gallery showing onto her. Lindsay wasn't like him, she wasn't like her mother, either. She had quiet ambitions—capturing a sunset, a misty morning on the dunes. He'd misunderstood that. Or rather he hadn't opened his eyes to who she really was.

Lindsay had a nurturing streak, not a competitive one. Hadn't he seen it in the way she worried about his supposedly ill body? Hell—he'd even encouraged that nurturing when it had suited his own purposes.

"I didn't think she'd told you all this—and she wouldn't have," Doc said. "And maybe I'm just a meddlesome old doctor, but I've always looked out after her."

"I...I needed to know."

"Lindsay's a very strong woman—what she had to cope with in her life proves that. But she's a vulnerable one, too. And that's why I don't want to see her hurt. Not again."

"I don't want to see her hurt, either," Josh said. He got up and stared out at the ocean beyond Doc's cottage. God, he didn't want to hurt her, but if he stayed, if he loved her, he was afraid he would do just that.

He feared Doc was right, he couldn't give Lindsay what she needed.

She would give everything to the man she married. And to her children. She'd be there for every school play, every soccer game, every swim meet her kids had, because her mother hadn't been. And Lindsay would expect the man she married to be there for her.

"I think I have a few things to think about," he said to Doc.

Numbly he thanked the man and set off toward the beach. He'd come to Doc feeling hopeless and he went away feeling even more so.

Josh paced off the miles along the beach, unaware of the tourists lazing there, the children building sand castles, the roar of the tide or the setting of the sun. He didn't know how many miles he'd logged. He didn't care.

The chill of the air alerted him that night had fallen. He jammed his arms through the sleeves of his Windbreaker against the cold as he sat on a rock, staring blindly out at the sea.

Only after some time did he realize that he'd unconsciously found the same spot on Folly's windward shore where he'd come with Lindsay the day they'd bicycled around the island. He'd kissed her here and told her they'd pretend there was nothing between them, if that was the way she wanted it.

But he could have sooner flown to the moon and back than he could have done that. Maybe he'd fallen in love with her then. He wasn't sure when it had happened. He just knew that it had.

He remembered the way she'd looked that day, windblown and beautiful, sweet and tempting. The taste of her lips, the soft tremor of them, came back to haunt him like a vindictive ghost. The warm feel of her in his arms threatened his sanity.

No woman had ever made him ache like this. He drew in a labored breath and let it out slowly, not knowing where he'd get the will for the next. His life loomed ahead, a bleak hope on his horizon. He searched the rhythm of the tide for solace, the darkening sky for repose, but found neither.

He doubted he could give Lindsay the life she needed—her island, its solitude. He doubted he could give her the part of him she would demand, the part of him she deserved.

He had a life on the mainland. He'd be nothing without his goals, his timetables, his drive, his successes. He'd petrify here in the slow lane.

He wanted Lindsay. He loved her with all the passion in him, but could he sacrifice his heart, his life?

Could he be sure he wouldn't fail her when she needed him most?

He shoved off the rock and began to walk again. He didn't know how long, he didn't know how far. The chill of the night deepened, wrapping around him. His thoughts, his doubts, his questions tortured his soul.

Until he knew the answers, he couldn't go to her, he couldn't hurt her. He couldn't promise her something he couldn't give.

Over the past two weeks Lindsay had baked every variety of pie in her repertoire—apple, peach, lemon, even marmalade plum. She'd baked enough of Aunt Rose's famed cinnamon rolls to open up a franchise. She'd cleaned every room in the Cottage Rose from top to bottom. She'd swept the front porch and front walk, mowed the grass and pruned the climber roses.

Today she was tackling the dust-laden attic.

It kept her mind off Josh, her hurt, her pain. It kept her from missing him, wondering what he was doing, if he was all right, working too hard.

If he was missing her—even a little.

She blew several decades of dust off a navy felt hat, a tired feather sticking out of the faded red grosgrain band. Aunt Rose's. She tried to picture her wearing it to church or to do the shopping in town. Finally she tossed it onto a prong of an old coat tree, where it dangled forlornly.

Why had any of this junk been saved? What did any of it matter to anyone years later? Moldering in an attic, forgotten.

With a deep sigh she glanced around at the collection of the past, everything from an ugly teapot painted with a geisha girl to old winter boots.

Maybe she would have a yard sale in the fall.

Fall.

Yes, the seasons would follow, one after the other, the way they had since the beginning of time. And with each passing season, Josh would fade from her mind. So would the ache that squeezed at her heart. So would her memories, the regret at what might have been, but it would take a very long time.

Under the small dormer window she found the old trunk Aunt Rose had always kept in a corner of her bedroom. Lindsay had wanted to go through it once when she was a little girl. She'd wanted to take out the old clothes and play dress up, but her aunt had told her there were things in there she cherished—memories, things from her girlhood—and had forbidden Lindsay to disturb them.

Lindsay crossed the room and ran a hand over the curve of the old trunk, then lifted the lid. Several old dresses had been packed away inside, the tissue around them brittle with age. Carefully she lifted them to find what might be beneath. What had been such a lure to her when she was a child tempted her still.

She found several old mementoes of the past, an old diary, some old family pictures Aunt Rose had shown her on occasion. Feeling like she was prying, feeling like Aunt Rose might catch her, she picked up the diary.

It was Aunt Rose's hand, a little more vibrant, a little more flowery than it became in her later years. She sat with her back to the trunk and read, forgetting totally the attic cleaning she'd come up here to do.

She read until the light from the bare bulb dangling overhead and the daylight through the narrow dormer failed her; then she took the old book to her bedroom.

The Cottage Rose was quiet tonight, the guests no doubt out for a late dinner or a walk on the beach. She had the house to herself.

She fixed a light snack and carried it, along with the diary, to her room. Plumping a pillow at her back on the bed, she began to read, but what she read stopped her, surprised her.

Aunt Rose had been in love.

Curious, she turned the page and read about the past, a past Rose had never told her about. He had been a fledgling lawyer in his father's law office on the mainland. In Boston. Rose had been spending the winter there, staying with her cousin, Emeline.

He had wanted to marry Rose, but she knew her parents would be expecting her back on Folly to help with the summer tourist season. They needed her, she'd written. Rose had been afraid, afraid to leave Folly and the life she'd known there for the uncertain life the man she loved was offering her.

When the time for her visit with Emeline came to an end, Rose packed her small bag, said goodbye to him and returned home, certain it was a decision she would always regret.

Lindsay wiped at a tear that trickled down her cheek.

Had Rose regretted it all those years?

Dabbing at another tear, Lindsay turned the next page and read on.

It was very late by the time she closed the book. She heard her guests return and go up to bed. She heard the old house quiet again, and in the quiet she knew what Aunt Rose would say to her if she were here. She had read it in the pages of the diary, read how Rose had hoped he would come for her, read how she'd ached to go to him, but feared it was too late.

She'd never forgotten him. She'd never quit loving him. The ache had stayed there in her soul, a pain so exquisite she couldn't share it with anyone.

Lindsay hugged the book to her chest and cried. She cried for Rose and she cried for herself.

Rose had made the safe choice, a choice that in the end had brought her pain, sadness.

The old diary was offering Lindsay a lesson from the past—if only she would listen.

Chapter Eleven

Lindsay glanced out the kitchen window to find a man sleeping in her backyard hammock. She nearly knocked over the pitcher of orange juice on the counter. Her heart missed a beat or two.

Josh.

The early-morning sun glinted on his lean, tanned face, ragged with the shadowing of a beard. His dark hair was wind-ruffled and tousled, his jaw slack with sleep. A rumpled blue Windbreaker and a pair of faded, frayed cutoffs were the only covering for his perfect body, curved to conform to the cradle of the hammock.

She rubbed her eyes and looked again to be sure she hadn't imagined him, conjured him up out of her need for him, her need to have him in her life again.

He wasn't some fuzzy remnant of last night's dream.

He was really there.

Her heart thumped wildly against her ribs. Her breath caught on the lump forming in her throat.

What was he doing here? Why had he come back? For a moment life stood still, for a moment she dared to hope.

Last night after reading the diary, she'd gone to sleep with a prayer that it wasn't too late for them. She prayed now. Prayed that he wanted her, that there was still a chance for them.

Coffee. The pot burped and gurgled on the counter beside her. He would need coffee, strong and hot. She reached into the cabinet for a mug and poured a cup, then started for the back door.

Rolls. Halfway to the door she thought about the cinnamon rolls warming in the oven, remembering how much he loved them. She scooped up two giant ones and slid them onto a plate, then hurried outdoors, padding across the dew-damp grass.

She stood at the side of the hammock and gazed down at him, aching to touch him, to curl up beside him and stay there forever, but she contented herself with just observing the rise and fall of his breathing.

Lord, but there was nothing more sensual in the world than a gorgeous man when he was sleeping.

His dark lashes fanned across the curve of his cheekbones, flickering lightly as if he were dreaming.

His breathing was slow and rhythmic, his muscles relaxed as if in exhausted slumber.

She stood there for a long moment more, looking him up and down and all over, savoring the sight of him. Every wonderful inch.

Wake up, Josh, she begged silently. *Wake up and tell me you love me, that you came back for me.*

He slept on.

She wafted the plate of cinnamon rolls under his nose and smiled when she saw his nostrils twitch at the aroma. He awoke with a start and bolted upright, making the hammock sway wildly. His dark eyes clouded with momentary confusion as he tried to figure out where he was and how he'd gotten there.

Then his gaze locked with hers, a solemn expression on his face. "I . . . I took the ferry," he said so seriously that she had to laugh.

"To prove that you could do it?"

He nodded.

"And did you sleep here all night?" she asked.

"Some of it. Mostly I walked the beach." He dragged a hand through his hair, a futile attempt to straighten it.

"I think you can use some coffee, and then we'll talk." She handed him the mug.

"Thanks." He took it eagerly.

"And a few rolls for strength."

He smiled and accepted the plate, balancing it on his leg. "Double thanks."

"You're welcome."

She sat down on the grass and watched while he ate, enjoying the way his mouth closed over each bite, his strong jaw moved as he chewed, his throat worked as he swallowed the coffee.

"I feel like a new man," he said when he finished.

There was nothing wrong with the old one, she thought, but said nothing.

"Can I hold you?" he asked so quietly, she thought she hadn't heard it. "Just... hold you."

She went to him, nervous, excited. Eager.

His arms went around her gently, making her feel as cherished as china. She felt the tremors in his body, felt his restraint. Her heart raced, like lightning across the sky.

It was to have been only an embrace, but Lindsay knew they were both crazy if they thought that was all it would stay. He looked at her softly, his gaze caressing her face, then her lips. Need exploded and in an instant he was kissing her like she'd never been kissed before. Hungrily. Needfully.

The roughness of his shadowy beard scratched against her face and she thrilled to it, wanted it, wanted him. She would give up everything for him— Folly, the Cottage Rose, *anything*—if only he would kiss her like this for the rest of her life.

"Oh, God, Lindsay," he said when he drew away for breath. "I walked the beach all night. I tried to put you out of my mind. I tried not to love you because... because I was afraid I'd hurt you."

She looked up at him, frightened, questioning.

He ran his hands over her cheeks, his fingers brushing lightly, memorizing the outline of her face. Her lips were swollen from the crush of his mouth. Gingerly he stroked them with his thumb, wanting to heal them, wanting to heal her of all the pain from the past.

If only he could do it, if only she would allow him to try.

"I was afraid I couldn't be the man you needed, the man who would always be there for you, the man who'd put you first in his life. I know that's what you expect from the man you'll love. Doc told me—but I think I knew, deep down in my heart, I knew. I knew you needed Folly. And you needed the Cottage Rose. I want to share those things with you, sweet Lindsay. I'll sell my share of the company, I'll move here, anything, so long as you'll have me."

"No, Josh, no." She was shaking her head, and Josh's heart sank like a scuttled boat.

"Lindsay—"

She put her fingers to his lips to silence him. "I can't let you do that. You'd die here without the challenges you demand from life, the competition you thrive on. Folly can't give you those things. And neither can I."

"What are you saying—that... that you don't love me, that you can't love me? I can change, Lindsay. I rode the damn ferry over here, just to prove to myself that I can do it, that I can slow down and smell the salt brine. I'll prove more to you, everything to you, just don't... don't tell me you don't want me."

She could never tell him that. It would be the biggest lie of her life. Aunt Rose might not have had the courage to leave Folly behind for the man she loved—for Rose, Lindsay felt sad—but she wasn't going to cry for herself.

"I'm telling you that you don't have to give up anything. I want to live with you on the mainland." She smiled. "Maybe I'll even try one of those gallery showings you want me to have—but just a little one."

Josh's breath caught in his throat. He felt like he was riding on the tail of a comet, Lindsay up there with him. "You...you love me enough to do that, to give up the island, the Cottage Rose?"

She snuggled into him, between the cradle of his thighs and smiled. "Only for you. You're the only man who could make me happy, the only man in the world."

No one had ever loved him that much, that completely. His heart swelled and he felt ten feet tall.

"Lindsay, I would love to have you with me on the mainland, but I've gotten rather attached to life here on Folly and its prettiest resident." He kissed her forehead, her nose, the soft curve of her neck.

Lindsay tried to ignore all his nuzzling little kisses and think reasonably. "It wouldn't work, Josh. You couldn't live here, you'd be bored within a few months. And you haven't lived through one of Folly's long, isolated winters yet or you wouldn't even be considering it."

"I can think of a few wonderful things I'd like to do with you all winter, sweet Lindsay." He dragged her into the hammock with him, making it lurch crazily.

She held on to the edge; she held on to him. He kissed her long and deep and thoroughly. She should be worried that the guests might be awake and peering through the curtains at them, but she didn't care if the whole world saw them.

He nipped at her bottom lip; his tongue traced its fullness, wickedly driving her mad. "Maybe we'll divide our life between both places," he said. "If I bring Folly into the age of fax machines and the financial channel, I could spend quite a lot of my time here. Summers definitely and maybe a winter or two marooned away from the rest of the world. Yes, I like that idea. How about you?"

Lindsay thought about it for a moment. She especially liked the marooned winters part. "This is all happening so fast, it's making my head spin," she said.

"Lindsay, I love you. As long as we want to be together, I know we can make this work for us. Marry me and make me the happiest man in the world."

Tears misted her eyes and she cursed them. She wanted to see his face clearly so she could remember this moment always. "I love you, too, Josh. So very, very much. And yes, I'll marry you."

He tightened his arms around her, loving the feel of her there. It felt so right, it felt so wonderful, it felt so perfect. "I promise I'll always be there for you, Lindsay. For you and for our children. Forever."

She knew it was a promise he would keep. She saw the fervency of his pledge shimmering in his eyes. She wriggled to better align her body with the hard length of him.

"Lindsay..."

"Hmm."

"Hold still or this hammock will dump us out. It's no place to sleep—or to make love."

"Don't tell me I'm marrying a man with no romance in his soul," she complained.

"You want romance. I'll give you romance." He kissed her, a wicked, naughty kiss that made her long for those isolated winter nights.

* * * * *

**HE'S MORE THAN
A MAN, HE'S
ONE OF OUR**

**MAD ABOUT MAGGIE
by Pepper Adams**

All at once, Dan Lucas was a father—and a grandfather! But opening his arms to his grandson didn't guarantee that he'd find a place in his son's life. And the child's aunt, Maggie Mayhew, would do anything in her power to keep Dan out of her family. But could she keep Dan out of her heart?

Available in October from Silhouette Romance.

Fall in love with our **Fabulous Fathers!**

FF1093

Fifty red-blooded, white-hot, true-blue hunks from every State in the Union!

Beginning in May, look for MEN MADE IN AMERICA! Written by some of our most popular authors, these stories feature fifty of the strongest, sexiest men, each from a different state in the union!

Two titles available every other month at your favorite retail outlet.

In September, look for:

DECEPTIONS by Annette Broadrick (California)
STORMWALKER by Dallas Schulze (Colorado)

In November, look for:

STRAIGHT FROM THE HEART by Barbara Delinsky (Connecticut)
AUTHOR'S CHOICE by Elizabeth August (Delaware)

You won't be able to resist MEN MADE IN AMERICA!

If you missed your state or would like to order any other states that have already been published, send your name, address, zip or postal code, along with a check or money order (please do not send cash) for $3.59 for each book, plus 75¢ postage and handling ($1.00 in Canada), payable to Harlequin Reader Service, to:

In the U.S.
3010 Walden Avenue
P.O. Box 1369
Buffalo, NY 14269-1369

In Canada
P.O. Box 609
Fort Erie, Ontario
L2A 5X3

Please specify book title(s) with order.
Canadian residents add applicable federal and provincial taxes.

Silhouette
ROMANCE™

The miracle of love is waiting to be discovered in Duncan, Oklahoma! Arlene James takes you there in her trilogy, THIS SIDE OF HEAVEN. Look for Book Two in October!

AN OLD-FASHIONED LOVE

Traci Temple was settling in just fine to small-town life—until she got involved with Wyatt Gilley and his two rascal sons. Though Wyatt's love was tempting, it was dangerous. Traci wasn't willing to play house without wedding vows. But how could she hope to spend her life with a man who swore never to marry again?

Available in October, only from Silhouette Romance!

If you missed Book One of THIS SIDE OF HEAVEN, *The Perfect Wedding* (SR #962), order your copy now by sending your name, address, zip or postal code, along with a check or money order for $2.75 (please do not send cash) plus 75¢ postage and handling ($1.00 in Canada), payable to Silhouette Books, to:

In the U.S.
Silhouette Books
3010 Walden Avenue
P.O. Box 1396
Buffalo, NY 14269-1396

In Canada
Silhouette Books
P.O. Box 609
Fort Erie, Ontario
L2A 5X3

Please specify book title with your order.
Canadian residents add applicable federal and provincial taxes.

SRAJ2

Silhouette Books has done it again!

Opening night in October has never been as exciting! Come watch as the curtain rises and romance flourishes when the stars of tomorrow make their debuts today!

Revel in Jodi O'Donnell's STILL SWEET ON HIM—
Silhouette Romance #969
...as Callie Farrell's renovation of the family homestead leads her straight into the arms of teenage crush Drew Barnett!

Tingle with Carol Devine's BEAUTY AND THE BEASTMASTER—
Silhouette Desire #816
...as legal eagle Amanda Tarkington is carried off by wrestler Bram Masterson!

Thrill to Elyn Day's A BED OF ROSES—
Silhouette Special Edition #846
...as Dana Whitaker's body and soul are healed by sexy physical therapist Michael Gordon!

Believe when Kylie Brant's McLAIN'S LAW—
Silhouette Intimate Moments #528
...takes you into detective Connor McLain's life as he falls for psychic—and suspect—Michele Easton!

Catch the classics of tomorrow—*premiering* today—
only from Silhouette

PREM

Silhouette Books
is proud to present
our best authors,
their best books...
and the best in
your reading pleasure!

Throughout 1993, look for exciting
books by these top names in
contemporary romance:

DIANA PALMER—
Fire and Ice in June

ELIZABETH LOWELL—
Fever in July

CATHERINE COULTER—
Afterglow in August

LINDA HOWARD—
Come Lie With Me in September

When it comes to passion,
we wrote the book.

BOBT2

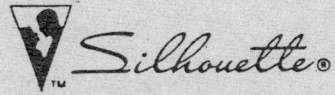

TAKE A WALK ON THE DARK SIDE OF LOVE WITH

October is the shivery season, when chill winds blow and shadows walk the night. Come along with us into a haunting world where love and danger go hand in hand, where passions will thrill you and dangers will chill you. Silhouette's second annual collection from the dark side of love brings you three perfectly haunting tales from three of our most bewitching authors:

**Kathleen Korbel
Carla Cassidy
Lori Herter**

Haunting a store near you this October.

Only from 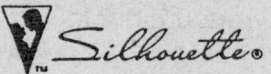 where passion lives.

SHAD93